BLIGHT

Winter 2015   DIGEST

Edited by

Bracken MacLeod

Ron Earl Phillips

Frank Larnerd

Jan Kozlowski

One Eye Press • Blight Digest

Table of Contents

Contributors

Horror is the natural reaction to
the last 5,000 years of history.
                    -Robert Anton Wilson

Horror is a Dirty Word

(FOREWORD)

BY BRACKEN MACLEOD

A recent article in The *New Republic* purported to tell its readers, "What It Says About You If You Enjoy Horror Movies." Its author drew a narrow, caricatured portrait of the typical horror fan: aggressive, unempathetic, male, and (most insulting) inclined to take added pleasure from his entertainment in the presence of a woman appreciably unsettled by the same fare. Perhaps most telling is that from the long history of cinematic horror to draw from, she singled out audience reactions at *The Passion of the Christ* and James Cameron's *Avatar* to illustrate her argument. Her unintended point is much more salient than her expressed position and is reminiscent of United States Supreme Court Justice Potter Stewart writing in Jacobellis v. Ohio:

> I shall not today attempt further to define the kinds of material I understand to be ... ["hard-core pornography"], and perhaps I could never succeed in intelligibly doing so. But I know it when I see it.... 378 U.S. 184 (1964).

Justice Stewart couldn't put a pin in obscenity other than to imply it is intuitive. The state of being obscene is largely subjective and varies by community and individual.

Between the lines of *The New Republic* article, the author tells us she can't define horror any better than Stewart could define obscenity, but she knows it when she sees it. Like him, she especially knows it when she doesn't like it. It's the thing that makes her look away.

That's not a minority view. "Horror" is a dirty word. When people like a vampire, werewolf, or psycho killer tale, they often call it dark fantasy, supernatural thriller, or suspense. When they don't like the experience of what they're seeing, they dismiss it as "gratuitous" or talk about "torture porn," as if that absolves them from having to explain why they don't like what they're watching or reading. It's the reduction of horror to obscenity—I know it when I *don't* like it. Even within the horror genre, there are people who claim to only like quiet or literary horror, but not splatterpunk.

Don't get me wrong, I like a good quiet story. The operative word, however, is "good" not "quiet." The common thread through all good horror—whether it be quiet, extreme, or in between—is that thing that pushes your buttons and makes you confront something uncomfortable like pain, loss, or your own mortality. It's the thing that makes you feel the titular emotion. Maybe that's responsibility, guilt, or unpaid debts. Maybe it's unexpected real world violence and blood. Lots of fucking blood. Whatever it is, it can't be dismissed because it's too strong a feeling. If you can snuggle up in it like your favorite warm blanket, it ain't horror. You might disagree. That's fine. It's art, not science. But I know this much, horror is a feeling. You feel it. If you don't feel it, it's not horror.

What I've tried to accomplish as a co-editor for two issues of Blight Digest is help curate stories that don't hit expected notes and merely provide fan service. I've tried to find tales of real dread with some element that made *me* feel uncomfortable (no mean feat). In Issue 1, the ones that really pushed my buttons were Kealan Patrick Burke's "Cobwebs" and Ed Kurtz's "Hungry." In this issue, I found myself unnerved by Eddie McNamara's "Serving Justine" and especially Matt Andrew's tremendous, "Farewell, Again." I am proud to present *all* the stories in this little digest. But I hope you are going to find in these pages, like me, one or two that go further, that push your buttons just a little more and give you that feeling like Justice Stewart described. You'll know it when you see it. And I hope you like it when you do. I hope it scares the ever loving shit out of you and makes you feel something. Really *feel* something.

And you know what? There's nothing dirty about that.

Farewell, Again

BY MATT ANDREW

Ready to officially record my thirteenth failure, I fire up the dashboard cigarette lighter. The previous twelve burns are still raw, scabbed flesh. Lined up in two rows of six along my thigh, like a dozen bulls-eyes, the oldest is just now healing into puckered flesh.

Today it's Ocean City Beach, Maryland. I'm sitting in my truck in the hourly-pay parking lot. The itch of my two-month old beard is maddening—salt and grit from Florida, Georgia, both Carolinas, and Virginia rubbing into my sweaty neck. Next is Atlantic Beach, New Jersey. Straight shot, about two hours up the highway. I'll sleep in the truck when I get there like always.

I know Danny's supposed to be resting forever at Largo Memorial Park, wearing his Pee Wee football jersey and clasping his stuffed panda in a stiff embrace, but I see him on every one of these beaches. Just a shimmer, skipping along the wet sand, leading me north.

Making me chase him.

● ● ●

Crumpled Filet-O-Fish wrappers cover the bench seat and floorboards—pale blue like a calm ocean under the pedals, rising into a swell over the transmission hump between the seats, then crashing over into the passenger side. Empty Yoo-Hoo bottles mixed in like messages from hopeless castaways.

That wrapper there, the one balled up baseball-size and tossed deep into the corner of the dashboard: That one was from Jekyll Island, Georgia, where everything had been going perfectly.

The dad was deep into the obsolete fifteen compressions, two breaths method of CPR. Must not have done it since Home Economics class. Probably never envisioned needing it for his son.

I stood there watching with the rest of the busybodies, ready to make my entrance. The scratches that the dying boy had clawed into my shoulders minutes earlier burned in the salt and sunlight. The cold, adrenal surge of an arduous task finally completed was flooding my body when another boy pushed through the crowd, crying. Same mop of blond hair as the one lying on the ground getting his chest pumped.

Turned out the drowned boy had a twin that I hadn't noticed while I staked out the family. Must've been down the shore, chasing crabs or something.

I left before the ambulance got there.

So, after Jekyll Island, I started canvassing families using the stick-figure decals in the back windows of their minivans and SUVs. The ones that advertise how many kids you have, whether you're married or divorced, what your cat's name is.

No more surprise twins.

• • •

That wrapper there, wedged between the passenger

door and the floorboard, the one with the smear of tartar on the corner: That was some shithole called Playalinda Beach, Florida.

I was finished with the boy and back up at my towel, but the parents were still motionless on their backs.

Any time now, the mom would get that internal alarm, the one where she's sensed that disconnect from her flesh and blood, that jerking pull back to reality that I'd already witnessed in Key Largo, Miami, and Cocoa Beach.

But, nothing.

So I walked over to them. My shadow fell over the woman. She had an assortment of steel rings pinned through her septum, ear lobes and lips. Pale skin covered in bright Japanese tattoos. Hair dyed so black it shined dark purple like an oil slick.

The dad was a snoring lump under a dingy "Stone Cold" Steve Austin beach towel.

I nudged her in the shoulder with my toe. Nothing. They both had that yeasty smell of body odor and last night's Jim Beam vomit.

Harder.

Nothing.

So I kicked the lady in her ribs. She coughed and slurred an angry sentence.

I leaned over and took her sunglasses off. Pinpoint pupils. Probably Oxy or something. She raised her arms in front of her eyes like she was Dracula about to combust from the sudden exposure. "Hey!" she said.

"Aren't you watching your kid?" I asked her.

"Aw, c'mon, man," was all she could muster. She snatched her sunglasses from me and fell back down onto the towel.

Why do I get to feel the pain while these people continue to crawl through life?

I stood and watched them for a few more minutes. Out in the water, there was no sign of their son's body.

Two hours up I-95 and I was still wondering if they'd figured out what had happened, yet.

• • •

Twenty-six sandwich wrappers. Thirteen bottles. Twelve circular burns on my thigh, like nickel-sized targets, ready to add number thirteen.

The truck ejects the cigarette lighter with a plastic *pop*.

I pull it out and take a deep breath. I bite down on my wallet, parched tongue sticking to the dry leather, and hold the lighter like I'm about to rubber stamp PAID across the top of my thigh.

Wait.

There...in the rearview mirror. Walking right behind my truck.

Freckles. Soft, reddish-brown hair. Spiderman bathing suit, holding Mom and Dad's hand while they swing him forward, off the ground.

No siblings or grandmas or dogs.

Just the three of them.

Probably headed to the beach for a quiet evening after spending the day at Jolly Roger's Amusement Park.

I look around the parking lot. Only one other car. The only sounds are sea birds circling and cawing overhead.

I seat the lighter back into its tunnel in the dashboard and grab Danny's towel.

• • •

There was a day when it was three of us, too. Before everything happened.

Me, Danny, and Sara.

I never called her Sara, though. We were on the swim team back in high school when I started calling her Betty, like the blonde from Archie comics. It stuck, even after we got married and had a baby. Even funnier is that I have red hair.

But that last day I'd ever spend in Key Largo, twenty-four Filet-O-Fishes ago, it was just me, eating our favorite beach lunch and sitting on Danny's towel while the birds pecked at crabs near the tide. A little girl knelt in the sand, making castles.

So, I sat there, wondering if Betty was happy, about as far away as she could get from me on the Atlantic coast with her new beach house and husband, and I noticed this boy, way out in the water. So far out all you could see was his little head bobbing up and down, his hair all spiky from the salt water.

Where's his folks?

Laying on their backs, working on their tans.

Their boy's out there, having to stretch his neck and look up because the water is past his chin and he's bobbing up and down to keep his nose above water and he's trying to see how far out he can go and I can practically feel the tenuous tight-rope he's walking way out there in the deep.

I stood up and took a few steps toward the parents, clenching my fists and taking a deep breath for the imminent ass-chewing they had coming. But I look out at that boy again and I stop, sand scorching the pads of my bare feet.

Danny's shimmering outline, ankle deep in the glassy

ocean tide, stared out at the boy, too. He looked like an old eight-millimeter film image projected on a billowing white sheet.

And the boy in the water, he had red hair, too.

Danny's ghost looked back at me. I couldn't make out his face, but I felt like he was waiting for me.

I could've warned the kid's parents, but it would've had a short shelf-life.

Instead, I swam out to the boy and began my journey north to Betty.

I know what happened to Danny wasn't her fault. It was mine. But we were meant to be together.

All three of us.

● ● ●

The Ocean City condos rise behind us like giant tombstones. The receding sun blankets their shadows over the quiet shore.

I follow the family onto the beach and look for somewhere to sit. Far enough to not be noticed, but close enough to be able to swim out quick if the opportunity arises.

I lay out the towel on the far side of an empty lifeguard tower.

The boy wades out into the crashing waters.

Mom and Dad are sitting in plastic chairs up near the dunes, backs against the OFF LIMITS barriers. They're shut off behind their paperbacks and floppy hats. The only other signs of life are a couple walking a dog, so far in the distance they look like conjoined twins holding a leash.

The anticipation of reunion makes my stomach quiver. Anxiety's cold fingers radiate down my legs from my crotch.

Their son's waist high now. He looks back at mom and dad with a silly grin and waves his skinny arms.

The mannequins that look like his parents don't notice.

● ● ●

Back in Key Largo, it turned out the girl making the sand castles was the boy's sister. She'd noticed that her brother was gone and woke her parents up.

It wasn't supposed to go down like that.

I watched from a white plastic beach chair while they escalated through the panicked-parent continuum. First you're confused—a jerky, short-circuiting robot with your mouth open but nothing coming out. You're looking around at everyone, wanting someone to offer up some bit of information that will make that incident a story you'll tell your son's fiancée two decades later over dinner.

You'll all look back and laugh.

Next, you discover through process of elimination, that he's not in the bathroom, he hasn't wandered off with any other kids, and he's not getting a Coke out of the machine behind the showers.

And last, you're grief stricken. The longest phase, it starts when you realize he's too far gone for CPR and the black pit where your soul used to be spans well past the day you're picking out the stuffed animal to put in his glossy hardwood casket.

So, at the beach there in Key Largo where it all ended (and started)—after the ambulance, family, and bystanders left—I went to my truck.

The cigarette lighter was a palette cleanser. A restart button.

No job. A few hundred dollars left in checking. An

eviction notice tacked to the door of our bungalow that morning.

The ambulance and police cars were pulling out of the lot when I noticed Danny back down on the beach, skipping through ankle-deep water.

Heading north.

I hit the highway in the same direction.

I knew where he was going.

Hampton Beach, New Hampshire.

Betty and her new husband, what's-his-name's house. Roger, I think (who's really named Roger anymore?)

With Danny and I making some stops along the way for posterity's sake.

• • •

I swim out toward the boy off the Maryland coast, a relaxed breaststroke through the foaming waves. I stop and look back. The parents are wandering down the beach, fingers linked in a loose grasp. The couple I'd scoped down the beach are clearer: an elderly couple walking a poodle.

This reminds me of Christmas when you're a kid and your stomach is buzzing from the anticipation of officially receiving the presents you'd already peeked at. My guts are twisting and looping.

The boy is circling in a lazy dog paddle. His eyes are closed but he's got this dopey smile like he hopes his dad will come out and see how good he's swimming.

He opens his eyes as I approach.

"Hi," I say. "What's your name?"

"Tim," he says, continuing his circles. "I can swim by myself now."

When he says that, I miss Danny more than ever.

"Thank you," I whisper.

Tim dogpaddles around me and I smile.

The couple with the poodle have walked past and are receding in the distance. Tim's mom and dad are crouched down, looking at something in a puddle of seawater trapped above the tide.

When Tim swims around me and comes back to the front, I begin flooding my lungs with oxygen. Quick deep breathes like I'm hyperventilating.

"What are you doing?"

I just smile while I fill my lungs for the deep dive I'm about to take.

Tim does another circuit around me and when he comes around front, I grab him and bring him into my chest. It's so quick he doesn't get a chance to splash or call out.

And we go under.

• • •

Some German guy holds the world recording for underwater breath holding. Over twenty-two minutes. You say you can hold your breath for three minutes while you're watching Monday night football? Big deal. Talk to me when you can do two minutes in the shallow end of a pool. The weight of the water is comparable to being buried in a load of wet concrete, squeezing your lung capacity down by one-third.

Back in my scuba-diving days, I could surpass ten minutes. Not even halfway to the record, but still respectable.

I haven't been timing myself this summer, but I usually only need two minutes. Just to be safe, three.

One boy—Jacksonville, I think—twisted and bucked for only about ten seconds before he went limp.

Folly Beach, South Carolina, though, the boy fought for a good four minutes. Taught me to fill my lungs more from there on out.

Tim fights for a minute, wriggling in my arms, trying to free his thin limbs and whipping his head back and forth. Not for long, though.

He leans his head against my chest.

This is the part I miss the most.

I loosen my grasp, closing him into an embrace. More of a hug than a death grip. I hold his head against my neck and my tears mix in with the salty ocean water.

It really is him this time.

A tidal wave of peace after twelve failures.

We hold each other there under the water, so long I almost forget I need to save some air to swim away.

This is the worst part, letting him go, knowing I'll never be able to hold him again.

"Thank you," I think.

I don't want to let go of him but his limp body starts to float away. The tide pulls while I hold onto his hand. Finally, a surge snatches his small fingers from my grasp.

I swim underwater with the cross current toward where my beach towel is staged.

The impulse to just lay there in the sand and cry as I'm crawling out of the water is so strong. But I can cry later.

It's not over yet.

• • •

The towel.

In Saint Helena Island, South Carolina, it came down

to the towel.

The dad pumped away on the boy's chest, hitting the American Red Cross's two breath and thirty compression sequence like a machine.

Mom, a tiny Hispanic lady in a red one-piece, is crouched low on both knees next to the kid, saying "no no no no no" over and over while she wipes wet hair out of the boy's eyes. She's leaning real close to his face, like she already knows it's the last time she'll be with him while he's warm and still hers.

Just like I remembered it.

Dad began to slow, shoulders and abs probably burning. Sweat trailed down the sides of his pale lats and dripped onto his son's chest from his forehead. Mom mumbled in the boy's ear.

Some old lady out walking a terrier, wearing a black one-piece with a frilly skirt and tennis shoes, stood there crying, holding a liver-spotted hand over her mouth. Her old man, sporting a fanny pack and blue-blockers, put his arm around her.

The high-pitched warble of sirens approached, floating over the dunes from Highway 17.

Dad faded fast, breathing like the tail end of a half-marathon, ready to turn it over to the professionals. Mom's crying rose in pitch.

I slipped through the circle of bystanders between two teenage girls.

The ambulance's scream reached ear-splitting proximity, and then shut off. Three men in blue coveralls crested the dunes and ran toward us, sand flying from each lumbering step in the deep sand.

Dad fell to the side, gasping, forehead planted in the

sand, back heaving from quiet sobs. His submission sent Mom's scream into the stratosphere. She looked up and wailed and all the gulls congregating at the edge of the tide flapped away.

I stepped forward, toward the mom while her scream sputtered out into a jerky groan.

I held out the Sponge Bob blanket. "Here," I said. "Wrap him up in this." I picked up her limp hand and tried to get her to take the towel, but she was in another world.

The Dad screamed and jumped toward me, slapping her hand and knocking the towel out of my grasp. He continued forward, barreling toward me with his broad shoulders like a linebacker.

"Get the fuck away from my son!" he screamed and before anyone could react he had me on my back, punching me in the eyes and face. I raised my hands to ward off the blows.

The grandma in the tutu screamed and the rest of the bystanders backed away.

"No! No!" he screamed while he punched my chest and neck. He was crying and his arms flailed, most of the punches glancing away or missing completely.

The two paramedics pulled him back by his arms and he still threw wild punches at nothing. Mom sobbed, runny with snot, still crouching by her son. The other paramedic checked vitals. His pokes and prods were slow, the habit without the urgency.

Blood ran down my lip and into my eye and my neck and shoulders burned from the wet punches that rained down on me.

Danny's towel lay there in the sand like the shed skin of some slithering beast.

So close.

Mom was supposed to wrap the boy in the towel, like a shroud.

That's how it has to be.

• • •

Tim's mom and dad scurry about, little action figures looking out into the water like they're expecting a ship to arrive.

Dad sprints into the water, leaping over the waves as they crash toward the shore. He dives, swims, disappears into the tide.

He comes back up, holding Tim in his arms like the boy's just asleep and he's carrying him to bed.

Mom's wails float across the empty beach. She's tearing at her hair and following them.

Dad runs up to the dry sand and begins what every father hopes he never has to do.

Two and thirty. Two and thirty while mom cries into her cell phone. Two and thirty.

I bend my head down between my knees and cry with her.

The old couple has turned around and is walking back toward them.

The heat rises up in my chest and I want to scream at them to get away, but I stand and pick up the towel instead.

I want to run away and I want to hug all three of them and I want to fall down into the sand and cry some more. But I keep walking toward them, towel open and draped across my forearms like some kind of offering.

The father, pale and flabby, has petered out of the CPR already. Mom is leaning over Tim's pale, smiling face.

I hand the towel to the mom. "Here," I say, "wrap him in this."

She looks up at me like I'm some angel come down to comfort her.

Mom wraps Tim up in the towel and holds him in her lap as the ambulance peels into the gravel parking area.

"Thank you," I say, but they don't hear me.

I get in my truck and I don't expect to see Danny's ghost again.

Eight hours to Hampton Beach. When Betty's slipping into the waves for her dawn swim, I'll be there, and I'll still be thanking Tim as I make my last dive, carrying me and Betty down into the depths to be with Danny.

Burrow

BY PAUL J. GARTH

Rory stepped inside the doorway, dropped the 30 pack of Natty Ice at his feet, and swiped the snow from his shoulders. His ears burned from the cold, and when he saw his hat lying on top of the old washing machine, he grew angry with himself for not remembering to wear it. He knew he was becoming forgetful, stupid even, and the knowledge of how quickly he was coming apart ate at his insides.

The wind had robbed his head of what was left of its buzz, and standing in the mud room of the rented house, he considered suggesting they do one more bag—just enough to take them through the coming storm—then kicking the shit for good.

In the living room, he saw Kirsten in front of the old moth-eaten sofa. Her jeans tossed over the back of the couch, she lay on the ground, her worn panties twisted halfway around her hips. She scratched at the inside of her thighs.

He stepped into the room and watched her scratch. A thin trickle of blood came to the top of her skin and spread over the pale flesh. Normally, the sight would have been sleazy and strange enough to turn him on, but her hair was dirty, her lips chapped, and from the tee twisting up and over her stomach, he could see a protrusion of ribs beneath gray skin. Even the slowly sliding blood looked unclean.

He felt a mingling of revulsion and sadness surge through him. He remembered the way she'd looked when he'd first met her, blonde and smiling with a crooked front tooth and green eyes that twinkled in the dark.

Rory wanted to tell her she'd changed. Tell her she looked burnt out and needed a shower—that it wasn't just her, even, that both of them were molting away to simple husks—but he held it in. He could get through another couple of days, and maybe, on the other side of the storm, things would set themselves right.

She looked up from the floor. "How is it out there?"

"It's goddamn cold out, but the snow hasn't come yet."

She eyed him between scratches. "Glad you got beer, but that's not what I want. We got any more?"

"I got a little bit left, yeah."

"Enough to get through this?"

He turned to the window. Snow blown from drifts slid down the glass, while the bones of the trees rattled in the purple late afternoon light. The baggie tucked in the pocket of his jeans felt suddenly lighter, and his heart began to beat a battle drum between his ribs.

His own cook had gone dry a month earlier, and in his desperation, Kirsten introduced him to the guy she got her stuff from, a tall man named Mark with too much energy for even a tweaker.

Rory didn't like Mark. Didn't even like the shit he slung. It was made with something strange, cut with something, Rory suspected, that would make him throw the crystal on the ground and stomp on if he ever found out what it was.

It tasted funny and made his body too twitchy to allow him to relax. Made him too sure of himself. Too reckless. And it did something else. Something scarier.

After smoking it the first time, Mark leering over his shoulder, babbling a load of bullshit about dark spots on the land, spots where other things had once lived, Rory realized this new shit made the world feel like it no longer bent at the edges. It felt like the universe hung at the rims of his eyes, and that, just past his vision, there was something else out there - something he could not see. It filled him with a sense of empowerment and panic all at once, and he'd had to bite the insides of his cheeks to ground himself back into Mark's shitty apartment.

"Yeah, that shit's helping you see, isn't it man? Is it taking you right back home?" Mark asked when Rory placed the pipe back on the coffee table.

The thought of smoking more, of having to go and meet Mark and listen to his bullshit about rocks and spirits and all the other lies, made his skin crawl. But his guy was still dry, there was a storm coming, and there was nothing else.

Kirsten resumed tearing at her thigh, turning the skin beneath pig pink. "Well, is it?" she asked.

"No. Not enough if it gets as nasty as they're sayin."

"We gonna be stuck here that long?"

"Probably a day or two. You know how it is. The roads won't clear out here too quick."

She raised her voice an octave, like a bratty teenager. "But I wanna get on," she said, drawing the last syllable out.

"Fine," Rory told her, promising himself that this would be it. "Call Mark."

Kirsten jumped from the floor. Grabbed her phone from her jeans. She flipped it open and hammered on the keypad. "It's gonna be so good, baby. I love Mark's shit. And after, I've got you all to myself. For days."

He watched as she pulled her jeans on, admiring her shape even though it'd lost some of its roundness. He imagined her naked underneath the sheets of the old bed. Their bodies buzzing and humming in sync with each other as their tongues clashed and they worked out their energy one last time. He smiled at the thought. It'd be like going out on a high note, and maybe after, they'd find a way to keep on without it.

The phone chirped beside her.

"Where at?" Rory asked, the smile fading.

"Bellevue."

"Jesus Christ. That's an hour away."

She slipped her feet into her old ratty Vans. "Then we better get going."

They left the house, wind beating down on them, blowing snow sticking to their hair. Inside the car, she pulled out the pipe and he filled the bowl with the last of their source. She turned the radio on then heated the meth. They took turns hitting it, smoke sliding across their eyes and down their throats.

When it was gone, Kirsten scratched. Her neck. Her arms. Ankles and elbows. "Fucking itchy", she said.

Rory slumped back in his seat and stared out the windshield, savoring the smoke unwrapping itself around his mind.

"You ever wonder what's up there?" Kirsten asked.

He turned his eyes up to the clouds, thick with waiting snow. He was aware of her talking next to him, but her voice ebbed and turned faint and musical. His eyes blurred, focused on the blackness at the edge of the clouds, wondering if anything lived there, in those places between light and dark.

Kirsten punched him in the shoulder.

"What?"

"Haven't you been listening? I said I was cold."

Rory tried to ignore the beat in his blood, then squeezed the steering wheel when it refused to fade. "Then you should have worn more than a hoodie."

She turned sweet. "Baby, come on, let's go."

"Goddamn Bellevue." He leaned forward and put the car into drive as the first thick flakes of the storm began to fall.

• • •

They slid over the road, the headlights of the Taurus doing little to light the highway. Snow mounted on the windshield as fast as the wipers could shove it off.

They drove, eighties rock and winter-weather reports filling the car, and beneath, the sound of Kirsten's nails scratching into her wrists. Back and forth. The skin turning puffed and red.

Kirsten didn't speak, and her scratching became a pattern, a rhythm in his brain. His foot automatic on the gas, the wheel gliding beneath his hands, his vision tunneling between the wipers and the snow and the dull headlights, Rory guided their course through the blizzard. The clock ticked off. His eyes glassed and straining, the sound of her flesh being torn raw in his ears. Time stood separate—a concept that applied only outside of the car and the pull of the tires on the snow and the sudden and growing fear that the edge of the earth stood waiting somewhere before them in the dark.

"We should be there by now."

Her voice startled him, brought his wandering mind back into the car. He hadn't been paying attention—had become trapped in his own thoughts again. He looked out the window and seeing the empty dark of the plains all around them, he realized they were lost. Between the snow and music and dark and smoke, they'd somehow gotten off 75, although he couldn't remember turning off the road.

"I'm not sure where we're at," he said.

The nails momentarily stopped moving. "How the fuck can we be lost?"

"Don't know. This shit's got me ripped."

"I know. But. Jesus, Rory. What the fuck? Get us back on the fucking highway."

"What does your phone say?"

She pulled it from the pouch of her hoodie. Flipped it open. "No service. God damn it," she said.

Of course there was no service. Even on the highway into Omaha their reception faded into nothing, and they had somehow gotten off of that. So why did he think there would be towers out here, wherever that happened to be?

"It'll be all right," he told her. "I'll figure it out."

Rory slowed. Tried to make out a landmark in the swirling black, but he was only able to see fence posts tilting on the edge of a field. He tried to orient himself, to figure if he'd gone west or east when they'd gotten off the highway. He turned down the radio and rubbed the fog-tinted windshield, but the stars were hidden fully behind the clouds now, and he saw nothing he recognized.

East, he decided. He would have remembered turning

across the opposite lane. It was the only way they could have gone.

"We'll get to the river if we keep going," he said. "Have to. We'll find our way from there." He inched the car slowly through the snow, his heart bringing blood to boil. A foul taste bled into his mouth and his ears popped, as though the pressure inside the car had suddenly changed.

Something buzzed past Rory's ear.

He stomped the brakes and held them, fighting to keep control of the car.

Rory tore a panicked look to Kirsten. "The fuck was that?"

Kirsten's eyes grew large at something over his shoulder. She screamed his name and flailed her arms at the buzzing thing as he felt it move towards her.

"What the fuck is that? What the fuck?"

The buzzing thing slowed and landed on the dashboard. In the dim light of the odometer, Rory saw it, black and large, with flecks of green in its wings, like a locust in summer. He wiped his eyes and stared at the bug, trying to convince himself he wasn't seeing shit that couldn't possibly be there. It was winter. All the bugs were dead.

Kirsten folded back in on herself. Her screaming stopped, but her fingers moved with the precision of pistons over her skin, drawing up lines of blood. The bug on the dash rubbed its front legs together, making a dull hum that filled the car.

Rory clenched his hands to fists, swung downward toward the dash and felt the bug crush beneath his hand.

"Rory, what the shit was that thing?"

"I don't know."

"It was fucking huge."

He reached down and wiped the bottom of his fist across the seat, smearing it over the fabric. He eased his foot off the brake. "Let's get the hell out of here," he said.

Snow blew in blankets across the road as he picked up speed. Wind tossed the little Toyota back and forth across the lines in the road. Outside, there were no signs and no mile-markers, not even a farm lit in the distance.

Beside him, he could see Kirsten's high was turning dark. Her fingers tore over her body. Her hands and wrists, her neck and chest. Tears shone underneath her eyes and blood sat mounted on the tips of her nails.

"Stop it," he said.

"I can't." She let out a rough sob. "Feels like something's tunneling in here. Bugs or somethin.'"

Anger pulsed in him, the urge to hit her tingled on his fingertips, raw and vicious. This was her fault, he knew, her junkie shit that got them out here in the first place.

He bit down on the insides of his cheeks and screamed. "Stop it, Kirsten! Stop that stupid shit now!"

In front of them, the road disappeared, pulled beneath a thick blanket of twisting snow. Rory slammed the brakes. The car shuddered to a stop. Kirsten let out a low moan and pulled at the sleeves of her hoodie, revealing more skin to scratch.

"Shit," Rory said, fighting the panic that had blossomed in his chest. The bug. The storm. The Snow. The smoke. It was all too much. "We gotta figure out where the hell we're at."

"Just take me home," Kirsten said. Her voice had gone soft and dreamy, as though her throat were barely connected to the rest of her body. She flattened her hands against her jeans, not scratching for the first time since they'd left the house.

In the dark of the car, her blood shone black and reflective, like the shell of something from the deepest strata of dirt. The blood pooled on her wrists and hands and neck, dripping across her flesh. "Just go back," she said. "Forget Mark. Forget the shit. Just get us home. I gotta get this shit out of me."

He watched as her eyes grew dark and rolled up into her head. Kirsten resumed scratching.

An image filled his mind. They were back at the house, snow tapping at the windows like it came from the ends of segmented legs. Kirsten stood over the sink, a screwdriver in her hand, prying skin and blood and muscle up and out. Tears trailed down from her bloodshot eyes. Over her cracked lips. A scream tunneled its way out her throat. He sat in a chair, watching, naked and scratching, while words he did not know flowed from his lips. The words in his mouth building to a crescendo, he watched as she gave a final tug of the screwdriver and something crawled forth from beneath her ruined flesh.

He kicked the thought away and eyed the trees on the side of the road. Somewhere in the back of his head, he felt the edges of the chemical fog lift before settling back down, but in that moment, the trees and the fields and the night rang with a twinge of familiarity, although he did not know how.

"You gotta calm down, Kirsten," he said, straining to keep his voice level and loving as possible.

"Can't," she said, her voice breaking between new sobs. "I can feel them. They're burrowing. Bugs. Trying to get to somethin' out there," she gestured out toward the window and the trees.

Behind her, he looked again to the trees in the field, twisting and bowing in the wind. Darkness hung between the branches. Something about the age and the blackness of the old growth, of the land, and every ancient thing buried beneath the black frosted earth called to him, an echo of his earlier remembrance, a feeling that spread over him at a slow pace, as though time were of no concern anymore. It made his guts loosen and his blood go acidic. Gooseflesh crept across his skin and mingled with the wild joy that swirled in his stomach.

Rory took a deep breath. Dug his nails into his own palms, cleared his head of whatever it was he was imagining. He reached over and grabbed Kirsten's furiously scratching hands, taking them roughly into his own.

"Stop it!" he yelled. "There's nothing out there. Fucking stop it!"

She laughed, a brittle sound, like breaking branches underfoot. "*Everything* is out there," she said.

He slapped her, the sound of the strike filling the tight interior of the Taurus.

Kirsten stared at him, words stuck in her throat, then wrenched away. She screamed and clawed at his face and drew thin lines of blood. Her eyes burning, a low growl shook from her throat that made his skin burst out in cold sweat at its strangeness.

"Get away," she screamed, her arms flailing at him. "Get the fuck away!"

She reached for the door handle. The overhead light flipped on as the door of the Taurus tore open in the teeth of the wind and Kirsten ran from the car, sliding on snow covered concrete in her slip-on shoes.

Rory jerked toward his own door, panicking at how

wrong it had all gone, then felt himself go rigid and im-
mobile in his seat. It was as though his own muscle and
bone were rebelling at the thought of chasing Kirsten into
the cold blackness of the night.

Bile filled his mouth. He leaned over the console, calling
after her as he watched her run toward the the trees. He
screamed for her to come back to the car. Screamed that
she'd die out there, that he loved her and he was sorry. But
she kept going, and soon she was lost among the trees, the
darkness, and the falling snow.

He slumped back in his seat. Let the breath, anger, and
guilt drain out of him. He reached over and closed the
passenger door, then stared through the window into the
trees Kirsten had disappeared into.

It was like she'd been swallowed up by them.

He felt something then, something moving beneath
the skin of his thigh. A quiver, a displacement, like something digging.

Rory closed his eyes and clenched his jaw. When the
itching faded, he opened his eyes again.

Snow beat against the trees and windows of the car.
He looked to his right, hoping to see Kirsten or the dull
red of her hoodie, but he could only see the trees. And
then, somehow holding a grip despite the wind and snow,
a large beetle skittered over the window.

He watched, horrified, as the bug reached the top of
the window and climbed onto the roof.

Rory shook his head. He knew it couldn't have been
real. He was hallucinating, like he had been earlier when
he'd seen the one inside the car. It was all in his fucking
meth-filled head. It had to be. But looking at the glass,
seeing the tracks the thing's legs left and feeling the guts

still sticking to his hand, he felt a coldness creep through his bones.

"What the fuck?" he said weakly, his voice breaking.

His thigh began to itch again. The tingling spread beneath the skin, moved inside the muscle, toward the surface of his leg, above his ankles, in his crotch and gut. He felt the itch pulse. A horrible thought appeared in his mind: It was as though the itch was communicating with something. Something outside.

Rory narrowed his eyes and watched the trees, suddenly sure that Kirsten had been right, that there was something in them. He stared, wiling whatever it was to move into the space in between the branches. To show itself. He felt its presence on the edges of his brain and the back of his neck, the surety of the thought terrifying and primal at the same time.

The pulse beneath his skin grew again, a throbbing call that rose and fell like something being dialed in.

The darkness moved.

A shape came forward, displacing the lightlessness of the trees. Black and twisting and hard, the dull glowing of the snowy night reflected from the thing's thorax, its segmented spine twisting and extending, the shape turned out of the dark, toward him, the contours of its head impossible and moving, its eyes casting a dull green reflection.

His fear wrapped underneath wonder, he found himself locked onto the shifting configuration of its form, the shape blotting away at the edges then returning again. Man and roach and worm all at once, fading and bursting until he stared into its eyes and only dull green existed.

Rory's mind fell back millennia, filled itself with silhouettes of worshippers, their bodies bleeding from erupted tunnelings. They twisted in a dance around firelight as the thing in the woods called to them and drew them close, its husked body glinting on the edge of the woods, calling out not to the worshippers, but to the things burrowing up beneath their skin.

Watching from the car, the shape took solid form again, but he could not look. Kirsten lay in front of it now, naked in the snow at the entrance of the thicket, a churning boil of blackness moving over her, cocooning her, erupting from her skin while the shape, shifting again, stood lord over her.

Rory screamed. The tear in his throat startling him enough to rip his eyes away.

His mind crowded and swirling with the shapes of insect legs and twisting spines and the silhouettes of dozens of green eyes, Rory fought unconsciousness by staring at the steering wheel. He traced the contours of the dirty silver Toyota symbol in the middle. He willed the haze of meth to descend again, begged for it to double in on itself and fall like a blanket and erase his memory. Rory closed his eyes. Flickered in and out of awareness. He screamed until his throat was raw. Then, hands shaking, fear electric on his skin, he reached up, and put the car in drive. He pressed the gas, but the tires only spun in the snow.

He opened his eyes and stared straight ahead at the road and the snow falling on the drifts, careful to keep the thicket from his sight. He turned off the headlights. In the new dark, he thought of Kirsten and the woods and the thing that waited for them between the trees, burrowing, calling to its brood hatching beneath their bones.

He felt the itching again, more urgent now, throbbing

everywhere in his skin. Rory looked down at his hands, then set the nails of his fingers to the flesh of his wrist, above their tunnelings.

Wind pushing against the car, snow mounting on the windows, the trees now just a dull green outline against the dark, Rory let out a low scream and began to scratch, and then to dig.

The Hunger, The Thirst

BY W.P. JOHNSON

When the outbreak truly destroyed everything and reached the point of no return, Sarah boarded up the windows with bookshelves and broken down chairs from a dining room set that she would never use again. The bay window in her living room was barricaded with the door from Tim's bedroom, the fake keyhole leaking daylight into the house. At night she hunkered down with a shotgun poised towards this sideways door, waiting for something terrible to claw its way in. When sunlight spilled in through the keyhole, it came in drop by drop at first, then the room slowly went from black to gray as the light began to seep in through the thin seams of wood, promising her another day.

Sarah set the shotgun down, her arms sore from holding the same position all night. She stretched and flexed her fingers, extending them into the slices of yellow from the rising sun. The missing nubs on her left hand shown gray around the base of lost fingers, the tips rusted with scabs and dry blood, faintly receiving the touch of morning through all the wrappings of pain.

She breathed in deep and cracked the joints in her shoulder. A cockroach froze under her faint shadow.

"Good morning," she said sarcastically. The cockroach

scuttled away from the sound of her voice, passing cloudy stains of dry blood and around a clean circle on the floor. It was where she usually set the bucket when she bled a fresh kill, keeping it out of sight when it wasn't in use.

She surveyed the other entry points in the house, making sure that the barricades remained secure. After doing a round of the first floor, she walked into the kitchen where the basement door was. A fridge filled with bricks kept the door in place. She scanned its perimeters, making sure that it hadn't shifted overnight.

She pressed an ear against the wall bordering the door.

"Good morning Chloe," she called out. After, she held her breath and listened, hearing a faint rustle from below, the sound of her daughter searching out her mother's voice in the pitch black of their basement. It was all Sarah needed to know that she was alive.

She left the kitchen and walked up the stairs to the second floor of the house. When she reached Tim's doorless room, she found him standing by the window, staring outside. It was the only window in the house that hadn't been boarded up completely.

"Good morning Tim."

He turned, slowly. His eyes were vacant light bulbs, spotted with the rustling flakes of beetle wings. His cheeks were sunken, his forehead distended with dark blue veins, a hollow shell of bone that looked hard and cold to the touch. A low groan came from his throat and he stumbled forward. She remained by the doorway, letting him approach. The jangle of chains sounded when he reached the threshold of the leash around his neck and he jerked back. Another moan left him and he clumsily felt at the metal wrapped around his neck.

"I know," Sarah said, nodding. There were no tears, only a pain that she hungrily consumed to stay awake. On the day that her husband Hank disappeared, she slept as much as she could. She thought about suicide, taking all the painkillers they had stolen from the pharmacy during the earlier riots, and let everything fade to black. Or maybe she could tie a string to the trigger of her shotgun and make death a quick painless snap of her finger. A numbness took hold, one that was making her slowly disappear.

It was the moaning of her children that slapped her awake.

She reached out and caressed his cheek. "I'm going to get you some food, okay?"

Tim stared, possessing all the thought of a house plant bending toward the light. When she pulled her hand away, he returned to the bedroom window and stared outside, watching a flock of birds flying south. He seemed to like watching the birds, likely because they were the only thing moving in an otherwise still sky. Sometimes Sarah wished she could give her children wings and toss them off the roof of her house so they could fly away. Then she could rest, could let herself disappear without the pain of her children's hunger slapping her awake.

But these were useless things to meditate on and she was wasting daylight.

She returned to the living room and checked her clothes. Some of the wrappings guarding her major arteries had loosened, so she undid them and started from scratch, making sure they would hold. Then she undid her boots and checked the wounds on her feet. They were purple and each missing toe was another nail driven into her foot. She doused them with alcohol, hissing to the fresh sting. After changing the bandages, she put her boots back on. The electrical tape over one toe was starting to rip where someone with the Hunger had tried taking a bite out of her. She had tripped over him walking through an overgrown field. If there was enough daylight, maybe she could try to scavenge for a new pair of boots.

She checked her watch. Eight o'clock. That gave her twelve hours. Ten if she wanted to be safe.

"Six o'clock," she told herself as if she were a petulant child.

Sometimes the Thirst made people desperate, braving the earliest suggestion of twilight or rushing out into the sunlight altogether when a thick cloud dragged its shadow across the ground. Usually, they screamed and smoked when they did this, rushing back to the safety of darkness, stinking of burnt flesh. In the cities, the Hunger was a slow mindless blob of a disease, lumbering its way through the surviving human population, but in her small suburban neighborhood, it was the Thirst that thrived as predators filled the night with the scream of lonely strangers.

Is Hank a mindless zombie hungry for my flesh? She wondered. *Or is he hiding in an abandoned home, waiting for the stars to shine so he can wet his whistle?*

"Six o'clock," she told herself again.

She stood by the front door and looked at the living room before leaving. The bloodstains on the floor were faint, too subtle to be noticed unless you were looking at them when the light was good. The clean spot where the bucket was left a faint blemish on her floor. Other than that there was only a single chair and a sunken in mattress that lay flush against the wall.

You could sleep, the mattress told her. *When was the last time you slept through the day?*

"No," she said, shaking her head. She knew that if she slept, her children would starve while she dreamed of all the things she would never have again because they were trapped in the days behind her. She chewed on some coffee beans and undid all the locks on the front door, opening it a crack and scanning her front yard. Everything was still as she rushed down the sidewalk towards the open street and an empty bag bounced over her shoulder along with the shotgun.

A military tank remained parked before her neighbor's yard. She remembered that being the first sign that things were getting bad. For a short while, journalists were reporting outside of the CDC in Atlanta where rioters were setting fire to the facility, wanting answers about some strange disease that was putting towns in quarantine. The Thirst had already jumped several states, moving at night. A strict curfew had been enforced. Broadcasters talked about the epidemic like it was a growing storm, using red to mark all the new outbreaks on a giant map of America. Georgia looked like it had a bullet wound in it that wouldn't stop bleeding and the bizarre plague spread further west, then south, cities overrun with the Hunger, the countryside destroyed by the Thirst.

They felt like it would never arrive. Then a tank parked across the street and that was that.

She walked up to the metal beast and pressed an ear against its side, hearing faint movements within, the rustling of hidden life. Sometimes she contemplated ways of destroying them, but the problem was too big and the three or four people hiding inside of the tank were a drop of water in an ocean of infected that roamed the countryside at night, searching for blood. She simply wanted to be left alone to feed her children. Hurting them would only draw attention.

She rushed down Mayberry Street towards a cul-de-sac bordering a steep hillside. A single man infected with the Hunger crawled about the hill, his legs broken and rotting. The wind filled her ears as she rushed past him onto the highway, masking the sound of his groaning. A massive supermarket lay silent across a traffic choked highway. She kept a safe distance from the abandoned cars as she crossed, avoiding the shadowy space beneath them for fear of having her ankle grabbed. When she reached the edge of the supermarket parking lot, she slowed her pace and approached the store quietly.

The vestibule was dim, riddled with old newspapers from a dead world. She kicked them aside and shifted the sea of words off the barren floor, seeing headlines like SECOND VIRUS SPREADS THROUGH THE MIDWEST and THE HUNGER TAKES NEW YORK CITY.

She crept about the supermarket with her head low, walking under the yellow blocks of sun that flowed in from the skylights. It was several minutes before she spotted another person. When she got closer to him, she could see that he was older, fit, with hard skin and filthy clothes. His duffle bag sagged off his shoulder from the weight of his possessions. When he turned to inspect a shelf, the rifle dangling off his shoulder turned as well, announcing its presence to her.

Damn it, she thought, backing away. She waited for him to leave, and every now and again she would poke her head up, finding him several rows down. At one point their eyes met when she peeked over an isle and he locked on to her. She held tight to her shotgun, saying nothing to the man as he backed away from her, leaving the supermarket altogether.

She sighed and made her way towards the front of the

supermarket, crouching by an opaque window that bordered the entrance. Sunlight bled through the plastic and obscured her body while figures that moved behind it would show themselves to her in blurred darkness.

"Don't fall asleep," she said, chewing on some coffee beans. When the caffeine wasn't enough, she kicked her toes into the ground, using the pain to slap her awake. She waited, trying to remember the last one she found. *Was his name Greg?* She couldn't quite remember because of how hard she tried not to think of anything at all when she was taking someone home. Still, moments would come back to her in flickering snapshots.

"*Got anyone?*" he had asked. It was what survivors always asked you if they found you alone. He had been in his early twenties, wore ragged clothes and mismatched shoes. His bag weighed heavy on his shoulder, nearly bursting the zipper with his possessions. Despite the world they lived in, he still shaved and put on deodorant, as if any day now things would turn around and he'd be presentable enough to work a normal job again.

"*Two kids,*" she told him. "*So far the house has been safe. Not a lot of food, but if you want, you can stay with us.*"

"*That sounds good,*" he said, smiling.

Greg could've been a friend. Maybe they could've made a run for the coast, found a boat and traveled to another country, found someplace safe. Instead she was slowly nodding off in a supermarket, waiting for a scavenger to come along. She was alone, using pain to slap herself awake. In sleep there was nothing but dreams and the things trapped in the days behind her.

Six o'clock arrived and tides of darkness started to creep in, pushing the safe shore of daylight off the parking lot.

"Ten hours," she said, groaning. She crept out the way she came, running across the parking lot. The only evidence of life was a small group of birds pecking away at a corpse on the ground, one that groaned beneath the blanket of moving feathers. They flew off in her passing and she glanced at the body; a naked man with tire marks on his back and a mouth full of beetles, his eyes two empty sockets. He groaned in her direction, as if smelling the meat on her.

She sprinted across the highway and climbed the hill to the cul-de-sac at the end of Mayberry, avoiding the same infected man that waited for her that morning. By the time she reached her house, she was out of breath and shaking. She looked up and down the street before unlocking her door and going inside.

As she stood there looking over her living room, she saw another flash of Greg, remembering how much he liked to talk like he hadn't seen anyone in a while. Sarah had played along with this, trading war stories with him, commiserating over all the people they had lost. All the while a single ember of her true intentions lay deep within her heart, one that she breathed upon lightly when the time was right.

Nice house.

The air was dim and the only thing he noticed was the sunken in mattress, the single chair in the middle of the room. His back was to her.

Where do I sleep?

She brought the hammer down without hesitation. Soon after, she dragged him by his feet and lifted him up onto the chair until she was able to wrap the rope around his legs, one that was tied around a rafter in the ceiling. She quickly pulled the bucket beneath his body and before he had a chance to come to, she took the knife and ran it across his throat, letting him bleed out into the bucket.

All of these things she saw while looking at the unmoving clouds of dry blood, the overlapping silhouettes of every stranger she brought home. The clean spot marked the bucket's place like a full moon filling one endless night .

A moan came from the second floor. A faint rustle could be heard below in the basement.

She looked at her left hand, counting the three remaining fingers. On her right hand, five fingers. Without hesitation, she took out the bucket and placed it before the chair. The knife clanged about inside. It was rusted with old blood and she wiped it clean with alcohol until the blade glimmered in the remaining light. Once it was sterilized, she set it aside and grabbed a water glass from the kitchen. Then she took a frying pan and cooked it over the gas stove, waiting until it began to smoke.

With the cutting board on her lap, she laid her right hand palm side up while her left hand gripped the blade with its remaining fingers. She mimicked the cutting motion several times and then counted to three, bringing the blade down. A clipped scream left her lips like an uncontrollable cough. After setting the cutting board down, she let the blood from her severed finger drip into the empty water glass. When it filed up several inches, she took a rag to the wound to stop the bleeding and walked over to the frying pan, jamming the fresh wound into the hot metal and filling the kitchen with smoke and the stench of burnt flesh.

A second scream took her breath. Then she breathed, telling herself that the worst was over. The wound was cauterized. She dressed it in fresh gauze and returned to the living room where she left the cutting board and the water glass.

She took the cutting board upstairs. The pain pulsated

and she felt her heartbeat in her missing finger. When she reached Tim's room, she felt faint but knew she could keep going long enough to feed them before going to sleep.

"Come here sweetheart," she said. She set the board down on the ground and he moved towards it, seeing the tiny offering of her severed finger. He placed it into his mouth and began to chew, groaning happily.

"That's it," Sarah said. "Eat. Be strong and healthy."

She left him as he fed, hearing his jaw click. She smiled to the sound of his feeding, knowing that he would not moan in hunger for the next day or two. She found the glass of blood in the living room and walked into the kitchen. It took her several minutes to empty the fridge of its weight so that she could shift it aside and make enough space to open the basement door a crack.

"Honey?"

A shriek came from down below followed by the thrashing of hands and feet as they raced up the stairs. Chloe poked her head out of the doorway, her teeth sharp and stained with blood, her pale face lit by the last shred of daylight that filled the house. When the light fell upon her face, she shot back, crying out as the stench of burnt flesh intermingled with Sarah's own.

"Chloe, sweetheart," Sarah said. "You know you need to be careful about the light."

The footsteps grew faint as Chloe crawled back down the stairs. Sarah knelt down to the floor and stretched her hand out, setting the glass of blood on the top step. After she closed the door shut, she called out to Chloe again.

"You can come up now."

Sarah pressed her ear against the door, listening to her daughter's cautious footsteps. Moments later, there was the sound of her drinking.

Sarah sighed, falling to the floor.

"You're okay," she told herself. She looked down at her hand and all the missing fingers. Someday there would be no hand, then no foot, and then no arm. She imagined that every severed part of her was a bird that she threw into the sky, letting it fly away, taking all her pain with it.

"You're okay," she said again. Her children were fed. She could rest now, rest and dream of the past, of all the good things trapped in the days behind her.

"Drink," she said, letting her eyes close. "Be strong and healthy."

How Little Sleeps

BY ANGEL LUIS COLÓN

It's when she's on the edge of falling under—
that moment when consciousness gives way to sleep—
it starts. The creak of floorboards above, the hiss of the
radiator, the rattling of the windows as a car drives by. It
didn't help the apartment was on the ground floor—the
windows double barred to prevent anyone from climbing
inside. In the distance, the cackling of strangers in the
alleyways between the tenement buildings. Nothing about
their laughter sounds happy, but these projects were not a
happy place. The girl wonders if those laughs belong to the
people who stalk the halls at night or the ones prowling
under the train tracks, pistols in their waistbands and
hungry for money. With all that noise, there are no police
sirens—never anything as assuring as the wail of a cruiser.

Her eyes snap open and she stares into the dark. It
makes suspects of the shapes around her—the towel on
her chair near the closet, the alien silhouettes that only a
moment ago were toys, makeup, and a stereo. The girl sits
up and lets her eyes adjust, slides from under the covers
and spot checks under the bed, and she moves to the window and double checks the latches. There's a sign right outside the window that reads, 'Bronx River Houses'. A gypsy
cab parked across from it with the interior lights on, but

nobody inside. A traffic light goes from red to green, but there are no cars waiting at the intersection. The source of the laughter is nowhere to be found.

The girl turns. Her little feet pad the cold, wooden floor. The familiar creak—three panels up and to the left of her bed—gives her some comfort. This isn't a nightmare, this is familiar. Content that the danger isn't immediate, she walks to the light switch and flicks it up. The single fixture centered above her bed comes to life, the decorative piece over the 60 watt bulb filled with a collection of dead insects and unexplained stains. Nothing—there are no secrets in the dark. She tells herself, maybe nothing will come this time. Her eyes follow the little black dots leading up the corner of the wall by the door. On the ceiling, the black spots congregate—mold—her grandmother always yells at her to avoid it.

A noise outside her door. The girl stands stone still and holds her breath. She listens to her heart beat—one, two, three, four— she waits until she counts to 40, until her vision peters out at the fringe before she breathes again. Her hand moves forward, grasps her doorknob, and turns. The door opens to the dark hallway of the apartment and the sound of her grandmother's snore. In the kitchen, the battery operated clock ticks and whirrs. The refrigerator hums and then grows silent. She walks to the kitchen and fills a cloudy glass with tap water. Sips it and stares at the sliver of bright light peeking in underneath the front door of the apartment. She hears someone buzzing into the main entrance and walking to the elevator bank next to her apartment. The elevator door slams shut, and the sound of the cable lifting the car fades as it rises to the floors above. She always wondered if the people on the higher floors worried about night time in this place too.

She finishes her water, and brings the glass to the sink. Roaches scamper away at her approach, taking a break from feasting on the crusting remnants on the bowls and plates left unwashed. Curious at the lack of response to her late night activities, she walks by her grandmother's room. Watches her shape rise and fall beneath a mountain of covers. A wooden Jesus hovers nailed to the cross on the far wall. The paint where his wounds are is chipped, white instead of red. He's flanked by two vejigante masks—the faces of the ancient demons her grandmother brought back with her from a trip to Puerto Rico. She claimed they kept evil away—that the masks were a part of their culture. The girl's grandmother told her they were ancient— powerful—a rare remainder from the times before Puerto Rico had been a victim of America's greed. The masks were noble, and would protect the homes of those that gave them shelter.

It doesn't feel that way. The masks feel out of place in the apartment. Their crooked eyeholes are empty, taking on the beige of the wall they're mounted on. Even the bright colors and crooked smiles do nothing to ease her. It's all a trick. There's something dark in them, the girl's grandmother would call it, *brujeria*.

Her grandmother shifts. Groans. Opens her eyes. "*Duérmase, pequeñita*," she mutters. "Go to sleep." Her Spanish accent thick and groggy.

She turns and heads back to her bedroom—back to the pinks and purples her family demands she love. She dives under the covers, opting to leave the light in the room on and her bedroom door open. Let her grandmother yell in the morning about the electric bill. A small price to pay for peace of mind, but maybe, just maybe—not tonight.

Her eyes close and she ventures to that edge again. This time, the sound of metal against metal. Her eyes snap open and the room is dark. Her door is closed. She sits up and notices her covers are now piled to her right on the floor. There's silence, the kind where the very air seems to hum.

"Not tonight," she says to herself and reaches to pull her covers back over.

They don't return to her, something has a hold and won't let go. The girl chokes back a whimper. She pulls once more, hears the sound of fabric tearing. The covers return, with a frayed corner. She wraps herself up completely.

Inside her cocoon, she can only hear her breath. Feels the warmth against her face and closes her eyes again— desperate to ignore the thoughts going through her head. Is it above her tonight? Under the floorboards? Maybe this time it lives in the mirror above her little dresser.

"Not tonight," she whispers over and over and slips back to sleep.

She imagines it in her closet, twitching and at the ready to pounce—all arms, nails, and teeth. At the thought of it, the covers creep away from her slowly, her legs exposed to cool air before something grabs her by the ankle.

She wakes up again. The bedroom light back on. A car horn honking over and over outside. The girl pops out of bed and runs to the window. The cab is still out there, but now the hazard lights blink as the horn goes off. In the front seat, someone is slumped over—not moving. The traffic light blinks yellow. The sign to the Bronx River Houses is upended and lying flat on the grass. Her breath comes ragged. The floor under her feet is hot, but the radiator is cold to the touch. She looks down and spots a patch of bruises where she'd been grabbed.

Her grandmother's voice behind her, "*Pequeñita*, sleep."

She spins on a heel and nobody is there. Her door is closed—her grandmother's *vejigante* masks now hanging on it—watching her. Her covers are neatly folded at the foot of her bed. Something scrapes at the window. She doesn't turn again—she's too smart for that—no, she runs. Desperately tries to open the door to get out, but its locked from the outside. Her door has no lock. She pulls and pushes. Kicks the cheap plywood paneling until the soft bottoms of her feet sting. Her cheeks are flushed and her eyes are wet.

"Not tonight," she whispers.

The door, by some miracle, finally opens. She scrambles out, a shadow looming behind her as light spills into the hall. Over to her grandmother's room, but there's nobody there. The windows are wide open and the honking of the cab's horn seems louder. Turning around isn't an option, so she ducks into her grandmother's bathroom, and locks the door. She grabs the doorknob with both hands and puts her weight into holding it closed, hoping this will hold whatever is coming.

She wakes up on the bathroom floor, curled up against the shaggy mat near the bathtub. She sits up and gasps. The bathroom door is open a crack. When she tries to stand, something presses against her chest and she's on her back again. The pressure is immense. She pushes against the ground, but her body feels so heavy. The bathroom door slams shut and the lights flicker. The faucets turn on. Hot water fogs the mirror and makes the tiles wet to the touch. Her hands slip against the cracked tiles as she tries to find a grip.

She wakes up in a sitting position inches from the front door of the apartment. Her legs are crossed. Outside, she hears banging against the walls. The honk of a car horn, the hiss of the radiators in the apartment going off all at once. She calls out to her grandmother, but there's no response. Someone laughs over her shoulder. She feels their breath on the nape of her neck. Feels cold fingertips trail down her arms. She turns and nothing is there.

She pads back to her bedroom and it isn't there. Just an empty wall—no door, no sign she sleeps here. There's no entrance to her grandmother's room either. Just a wall, cold and white. She runs a hand over where her doorframe would be and the paint chips away. Before long, there's a snowfall at her feet. Beneath the white, black. It shines like opal—like the rings her mother used to wear. Heavy footsteps sound behind her, but she knows not to turn. When she turns, they win. Something scrapes on the floor—like heavy furniture being moved. The buzzer at the main entrance sounds off, but doesn't cease.

"I won't let you do it. Not tonight."

The girl presses her hands against the wall and closes her eyes. She gently knocks her forehead against the wall. The dull thud carries around the room. Something knocks back. She's had enough. Wills herself to wake up on her bed in a lit room, in a cocoon of blankets, and with her door open. "Please not tonight. Just let me sleep one night."

Her prayer remains unanswered.

The shadow of it bears down over her. It's right behind her. Close enough to send a whisper of cold air across the hairs on her neck and back. Close enough to weigh her down again—to make her breathing short and her heart pound against her chest like a taut drum. For the first time, she wants to wake up anywhere else but there. The tears come again, but she won't turn. Not again, not like last time. She knows the cold of it, the nature of its embrace.

Something grips her forearms—hard—but she won't turn. Ice water runs down her spine and down her legs. Warm liquid flows through her hair and down her face. It drips from her chin. She fights the urge to wipe herself clean. She smells pennies and tastes them at the back of her throat. "*Duérmase, pequeñita.*" The voice is nails on a chalkboard, a cold gust of wind through dead trees, the buzzing of a million flies at once. It turns her roughly. Caresses her face with razor nails. She feels heat where it scratches her cheek.

"*Pequeñita,*" it rasps.

It pulls her off her feet and into a tight embrace. It coos, comforts her, and assures her that it will be over once she looks. All she has to do is look. All she has to do is let it feed. The flesh of its hands is smooth and smells of summer: hose water, grass clippings, and chocolate. It continues to whisper about her favorite food—fried chicken—and her very favorite dress. All the good things it knows about already. It wants more of that, more of what makes her happy and comfortable in these run-down projects by the dirty Bronx River. What's left behind is coal—hardened and black. It reminds her that will be what it takes to stay here and to survive.

She nods and smiles without joy. Opens her eyes and falls into the dark.

On Dark Wings

BY TONY WILSON

Gin studied the silver badge on the Captain's desk. A bald eagle adorned the top, clutching a banner in his talons bearing the words PROTECT & SERVE. Below its wings were engraved the City of Cactus Springs official seal and the number 86 – her number. She reached out to touch it and then thought better. It had been months since she'd worn it. Those memories felt like they belonged to someone else.

Captain Davis grunted to himself as he thumbed through Gin's personal file. Bloodshot yellow eyes glanced at her over the top of the folder. If there was judgment behind those eyes, she couldn't read it. His brow didn't crease, nor did she detect an arch of the eyebrows. Davis was stone-faced as usual.

The smell of coffee and nicotine barely masked his stale breath. "I've read the report from the doctor. She thinks you're ready for active duty. I'm still on the fence. What do you think?"

She chose her words carefully. "I need this, Sir. The structure will be good for me. I'm sure the doctor agrees that sitting at home isn't going to help me… get on with things."

He nodded. "Do you really believe that, or are you just

telling me what you think I want to hear?"

"I'm doing about as well as you'd expect. Every little sound still wakes me up at night, thinking it's going to be him coming home... or worse."

She looked away before her eyes started to well up and nibbled on her thumbnail.

"Virginia, I know you're hurting in ways I can't even imagine," he began. "I can go through all the rah-rah bullshit about how you're a great cop and we're just like family here, but I know that's not your thing. Just know that if you need someone to talk to, I'm here."

She pocketed the badge and offered Davis her hand. "Thank you, sir."

He shook it firmly. "I'm putting you on mids. Briefing is at nine p.m. sharp. You can get some shuteye during the day; no nightlights necessary."

• • •

The dreams were always a variation on the same series of events. She heard the noise downstairs and grabbed a sleeping mask instead of her service pistol. She looked back at Joel, sleeping upside down on the bed, with his feet on the pillows. Another thump downstairs. She turned around and found herself at the bottom of the carpeted stairs. She looked at the sleeping mask in her hands, pink and fluffy, like something a wealthy oilfield wife would wear. She sneered at the mask, but still slipped it on.

In this dream, she could see through the mask, into a rose-colored haze. Another thump led her through the living room and into the study where the man would be. His sickly-sweet smell turned her stomach as she entered the room.

There he was – the junkie with the gun. He mumbled something unintelligible and pulled the trigger.

Her eyes snapped open and another thump echoed in her head.

"Watson, you okay?" Officer Blake knocked on the car window again. "Chow time's over, kid. Dispatch is looking for you."

She shook the cobwebs out of her head and squeezed the steering wheel. "Shit. Thanks. Still getting used to the schedule."

Blake laughed and headed back to his unit.

The lies came a lot easier these days, her best method of self-defense against uncomfortable discussions or looks of pity. The truth was, antidepressants made her sleepy. Gin knew she wasn't ready to be back on duty, but she desperately needed an anchor to the real world. She was tired of tears. Work pushed the grief aside, and let her focus on something else, be a part of something.

Another knock on the window kept her from drifting off.

"I'm awake, Blake. It's all—"

She turned her head to the window and teenage boy, maybe 14 or 15, stood there, hands shoved in his pockets. Gin looked for a skateboard under his arm or a BMX bike behind him, common sights when dealing with the little shits around town. But it was just him, standing there with a wide-brim cap pulled low.

She pushed the button and rolled the window down a couple of inches. "You looking for a ticket for being out past curfew?"

His eyes, shadowed under the brim of the cap, stared through her, making her uneasy. She wasn't used to feeling that sort of fear. Joel's death had changed that, chipping away at the brave front she put up when on duty now.

"I need a ride," said the boy in a monotone. "Give me a ride?"

Give me a ride. Was he asking or demanding? There was an edge beneath the words that stirred up something inside her. It didn't sound like a threat, but it felt like one.

"Sorry, kid. I'm busy," she answered. "Try Coyote Cab. Probably one outside the bars down the street."

"I need you to drive me home. I'm late and my family is worried."

Gin reached down to roll up the window, but found her fingers resting on the button for the door lock. "I…"

The radio crackled to life. *"Cactus Springs 86."*

She grabbed the mic from its holder on the dashboard. "This is 86. I'm at Queen and 6th. Go ahead."

"27 requests assistance at Grace and 14th with a disorderly female."

"Copy that. Put me en route."

Gin turned to tell the kid to go home, but he was already gone.

• • •

The Oasis Club was a popular bar downtown on 14th street. A giant neon cowboy hat hung askew from the top of a smiling cactus on the front of the building. They brought in Tejano bands on the weekend, which in turn brought out the locals dressed in their finest western wear. The number of unironic mustaches and cowboy hats in town had taken some getting used when Gin and her husband first moved to town.

She pulled into the alley behind Blake's squad car and

checked in. "86 I'm 10-23."

She tugged on her black CSPD cap and headed inside to see what Blake had gotten himself into.

The show was in full swing with the headlining band standing in front of a twelve foot video wall built from a stack of monitors. Colored lights spun across the dance floor while the singer told a story about his first love. At least that's what it sounded like to Gin. Her Tex-Mex wasn't all that great, but at least her Germanic roots allowed her to enjoy the accordion.

Officer Blake stood over a thin Hispanic woman who had attached herself to a railing that divided the main bar from the dance floor. She mumbled incoherently from under a tangled mess of long black hair hanging over her face. Her short dress crept up the sides of her hips so anyone interested could get a good look at her Hello Kitty panties. Blake tried to reason with her, to get her to stand up, but she didn't want to leave yet.

"C'mon now, girl. You're embarrassing yourself. Just let me help you up," he said in his friendly southern drawl.

Gin elbowed the tall man in the ribs. "You're supposed to be working, not looking for a date. Does your supervisor know about this?"

"Ha ha. I need your help with this young lady. She's refusing to leave and there's no way in hell I'm going hands-on with a damsel in distress."

Gin hunkered down, bringing herself down to eye level with the woman. "Looks like you've had a rough night, sister. Let's get you in my car and I'll take you home. Lot of creepers in here and you are in no shape to fend them off."

She stuck out her hand, but the woman just shook her head and rattled off some drunken Spanish.

"No habla Español. Let's get you out of here."

"No! I'm not going home. I can't." the woman pleaded, this time in English.

Gin carefully placed a hand on the woman's arm. "What's going on at home? Did somebody hurt you? Husband? Boyfriend? I can call the women's shelter and find you another place to stay for a few days, but I'll need you to press charges if you want this to stop."

"No, I live with my sister."

"Where is your sister now?"

"She is visiting friends in San Antonio," the woman mumbled.

"The club is going to close in half an hour, so you can't stay here," Gin explained. "I'll tell you what. I'll take you home, but we'll take the long way. You can ride around with me for a while. When you're feeling a little better, we'll get you to bed. Deal?"

Blake whispered in her ear. "Are you sure about that? This is at least the third time we've had problems with her this week."

Gin nodded. "She'll pass out in five minutes and I'll drop her off. Problem solved."

The woman stretched out a hand and the two officers carefully pulled her to her feet. Gin took notice of the track marks on her arm. They were healing, but not more than a week old.

Blake gave her a wave and strolled back into The Oasis for another walk-through. He was one of the good ones, Gin thought, keeping an eye on the crowd as they stumbled outside. He liked to make sure that everyone who needed a ride got one. As long as you weren't belligerent or deluded about your condition, he'd make sure you got home in one piece. If you gave him lip though, you were in for a long night.

Gin helped the woman into her squad car, placing her in the front seat instead of back in the cage. She dropped into the driver's seat and grabbed the mic from the dash.

"Cactus Springs, this is 86."

"Go ahead."

"I'm leaving the Oasis Club now. Going 10-8"

"Copy that."

Her passenger fidgeted about, pushing her face up against the window. Gin cleared her throat. "Got a name?"

The girl nodded. "Maya."

"Officer Watson, but everyone calls me Gin. Where am I dropping you off?"

"527 1/2 Shelby."

"Want to tell me about the holes in your arms?"

"I can't stay clean," Maya turned to face her, her eyes wet with tears. "But I have to."

"Want to or have to?"

"Have to. I overdosed last week. Cardiac arrest," she sniffed. "I think I… died."

Gin shook her head. She hated these kinds of situations. She never knew what to say. "What makes you think that?"

"I saw myself… from above. I was in the emergency room on a table."

Gin pulled the car into an empty parking lot and set the parking brake. She took a deep breath, wondering why she was sharing her own story with a stranger. "My therapist told me that was normal. Just synapses firing in your oxygen-deprived brain. Like a dream."

Maya's eyes widened. "You've seen it too then? What

happened?"

"A man shot me. I heard some noise downstairs in my home, so I went down to have a look. I was smart enough to take my gun with me, but… he got the drop on me. He left me to die while he went upstairs to loot the rest of the house. I passed out from all the blood loss, but I heard another shot as I drifted off." Gin blinked hard. "My husband… he didn't make it."

"I'm so sorry," Maya squeezed her arm.

"I finally got back to work and I want everything to just be normal again. But it can't be. I can't even talk to anyone at the office about this. I hate the way they look me at me. Like I'm… broken." She wiped away the tears with the back of her hand. "A part of me did die back there. I'm not even sure anymore if it's worth living without it. I was too stubborn. I should have just…let go."

Gin rubbed her nose and fished a tissue out of the center console to dab her eyes. She beat the steering wheel with her fists, angry at her emotions. Her hand went for another tissue and she saw that Maya was slumped down in the seat, passed out.

• • •

527 ½ Shelby Street was nothing more than a tiny garage converted into an efficiency apartment in the alley. Peeling paint dotted the shack that might have once been blue. The porch light had long since been smashed and no one bothered to replace it. It was a part of town where you didn't worry about being robbed because you didn't have anything worth taking to begin with.

Gin helped Maya shuffle to the front door.

"Almost there. Got your key?"

Maya gave her a slow nod, like a little kid who had been asked if they were sleepy. She flipped the top of the rusty mailbox open. Gin shone her flashlight inside and grabbed the lone key. She opened the door and felt along the wall inside for a light switch. The bulb dangling in the center of the room flicked to life.

The apartment looked even worse on the inside. An old twin bed buried under a pile of clothes sat in the far corner. It wasn't even sitting in a frame, just a mattress on box springs. The cheap tile floor curled up in several places. The walls were a dingy yellow; someone had spent a lot of time in that room smoking like it was their job.

Gin guided the girl to the bed and shoved enough of the clothes aside to make a place for Maya to lie down.

"You good?"

Maya rubbed her eyes. "Please don't leave."

"I have to get back on patrol. Drink some water and get some sleep. Everything will be better tomorrow," Gin said.

She dropped the house key on the bedside table, noting a trio of black candles. They were the kind sold in the Mexican grocery stores. She picked one up and sniffed it. It had been burning earlier.

"No, you can't leave me. They're watching."

Gin turned toward the door so Maya couldn't see her roll her eyes. "No one's watching. Go to sleep."

"I can hear them outside… whispering."

"I'll have a look around before I head out, okay? Good-night, sister."

Gin locked the door and closed it behind her. She rattled the handle a few times to make sure it was secure. Satisfied that she'd gotten the girl home safely, she headed back to her unit.

Her fingers brushed the door handle and she paused. While on patrol, she spent a lot of time cruising around with the windows down. It was easier to hear what was going on in a neighborhood. She'd become accustomed to the sounds and even smells of Cactus Springs. As she stood by the car, the only noise she heard was the humming of the engine. No breeze. No birds or crickets. Nothing.

At the other end of the alley, something skidded to a stop on the loose gravel. Gin squinted, trying to make out the silhouette backlit by a security light on the next block. It was a kid on a bike.

"Its way past curfew, you know," she said.

The silhouette stayed frozen, head cocked to the side.

She pulled open the door and reached for the spotlight. Her thumb pressed the switch. The light flickered and popped.

"Really?"

The car groaned as she slid into the driver's seat and slammed the door. Instinct told her to check in with Dispatch, but the only traffic on the radio was crackles of static. Up ahead, the figure moved, rolling toward her. Gin closed her eyes, swore again, and gripped the wheel.

"Get your head straight, girl. You're jumping at shadows."

The engine sputtered and died. When she opened her eyes, the headlights and interior lighting were out, leaving her in complete darkness.

Someone tapped on the passenger window. Gin pulled her gun and stared at the window, trying to see who was out there. Another tap came from behind her on the driver's side. She whirled in her seat to face the new threat. Something heavy pounded on the roof of her unit, alternating sides, rocking the car violently from side to side. A rain of blows came crashing down on the hood, like a sudden hailstorm that ended as quickly as it began.

The strange game continued until a cacophony of sounds surrounded her in the vehicle. Gin turned the key. The car refused to turn over. She tried again, screaming at the dashboard in front of her.

Outside, the pummeling abruptly ceased.

She turned the key again and her unit rumbled to life. The headlights pierced the darkness of the alley. No one was there. The only thing she could make out was a line cut in the gravel by bicycle tires.

● ● ●

It took a few days, but curiosity got the best of her. After wrapping up her paperwork from her shift, Gin decided to pay a visit to Communications. Alberto looked up from his iPad, embarrassed at getting caught.

"I uh…"

"Don't give a shit, Al. I didn't see anything. I need you to pull up some reports for me though."

Alberto pushed his chair over to his workstation and awaited her request.

"Do you remember any recent calls from a girl named Maya over on Shelby Street?"

He grinned. "Oh yeah, we know Maya. That girl has issues. How far do you want to go back? And do I even want to ask why?"

"Nope. How about two weeks?"

"Give me a few minutes and I'll get those printed for you."

"So, she calls a lot?"

"Real paranoid type. She's a heroin addict, so what do you expect. Lives with her sister. Maya's always calling in about suspicious persons."

"Yeah, I got that vibe the other night when I drove her home from the Oasis. She was worried about being watched. Is the sister around much?"

"Not really. Day shift tells me she checks in every few weeks, pays the bills, and goes back to doing her own thing."

A couple dozen pages came rolling out of the printer. Gin grabbed the papers and thumbed through the stack.

"This is crazy. Look at all these CAD numbers."

Alberto chuckled. "I told you. It's gotten even worse this week. The big overdose drama has her working the phones overtime."

"She really did OD?"

"I heard they almost lost her. Now she's back and more loco than ever," Alberto said. "That girl is gonna flame out soon."

She nodded in agreement. "I drove her home the other night. Haven't been able to get her out of my head."

"Sometimes it's hard to keep your distance in this line of work. There are a lot of lost souls out there and you can't save them all."

• • •

Her dreams were besieged by images of Maya. Her presence was inescapable. The girl and her long black hair would be standing off to the side of every scene, whispering. Every time Gin got close enough to make out the words, Maya would dissipate, like a cloud of smoke pulled apart by a breeze.

The alarm went off and by the time Gin had rubbed the sleep out of her eyes, she had talked herself into stopping by Shelby Street for an unofficial visit. Someone else had taken up residence in her head and it was time to figure out why.

It was the middle of the afternoon and the unrelenting south Texas sun threatened to roast Gin in her car. She rolled the windows down with one hand while cranking up the AC with the other. The silver shade in the front window was fighting a losing battle. She tossed it in the backseat and pulled out of the driveway.

She pulled into the gravel alley. The ramshackle building looked even worse in the daylight. Surprisingly, the overeager city inspectors hadn't condemned it. Gin knocked on the front door and waited.

"Maya, it's Officer Watson from last week. I just want to talk. Can I come in?"

Nothing.

She tried the knob. It turned effortlessly.

"I'm coming in, okay?"

The door creaked open and the smell hit her like a punch to the gut. It was a mixture of sweat, feces, and rotting meat, baked in the sweltering heat with nowhere to escape. Gin vomited into the scrub grass outside. After a few dry heaves, she collected herself enough to step inside.

Maya was crumpled in the loveseat, like a ragdoll cast aside by a child. The heat had fused sections of her skin with the faux-leather chair. It had pulled away in strips as the body sagged. Her once glossy black hair was now brittle and gray. Her face was a twisted mask of terror with her mouth gaping wide and two milky white orbs splashed with red staring into nothingness.

"No, no, no," Gin said.

Her first instinct was to look for needles, but this didn't fit the characteristics of a heroin overdose. She looked at the husk that used to be Maya. This was something else entirely.

She pulled out her phone and dialed the station.

• • •

Captain Davis leaned back in his chair and gave her his best "I'll wait and let you say the wrong thing first" look.

"I was off duty and driving my own personal vehicle," Gin said.

He stared hard at her. She might as well be playing poker with a brick wall. "So? I was on duty and sitting at my own desk. My concern is what were you doing at a known drug abuser's residence?"

"It's all in my report. Captain, no one was as surprised as me to find her like that. I drove her home from the Oasis last week and I felt…sorry for her."

"Why'd you return to the house?"

"I heard that she'd been keeping Dispatch busy with calls. I was hoping I could talk her into getting some help."

"And that's all there is to it?"

Gin was lost. "Yes, sir."

The Captain dropped a stack of papers on the desk in front of her. Someone had meticulously highlighted several lines on every single page in yellow. She pulled the stack closer, scanning the first page to see what was so interesting.

"Why didn't anyone tell me about this?" she asked, rifling through the pages.

He sat there stone-faced.

"C'mon, Captain. These are the drug-addled ramblings of a woman on the edge."

He snatched the papers out of her hands. "*I need to speak to Officer Watson. I've heard them outside. They said her name again.*"

"I don't know who *they* are."

"*They're pounding on the door again. I want to let them in, but I can't. Tell Officer Watson.*"

"She was…obsessing over me. I can't help that."

"*Did you give my message to Officer Watson? They're coming for her.*"

A cold chill crept up Gin's spine. "Sir, I really have no idea what she's talking about."

"*Madre de Dios! She's next. Tell her she's next.*"

Davis dropped the stack on his desk and massaged his temples. "Watson, if you're in some kind of danger, I need to know. This is not the time for secrets. I don't care if it's something you did off duty."

She pushed her hair back out of her eyes and met his gaze. "Sir, there is absolutely *nothing* going on. I'm not in any danger that I'm aware of. When I get off work, I go home to sleep. In the afternoon, I work out or run. I have no social life. Our old friends don't come around to visit anymore since I became the odd one out. Sometimes I just sit in his old recliner in the living room and cry. That's it. That's poor little Virginia Watson with her new fragile existence. Don't make any sudden moves or she might start sobbing again. I'm a pariah now because apparently I'm not the only one who doesn't know how to move forward."

Davis sat in stunned silence.

"Maybe things would be easier for everyone if I'd bled out."

"Do you think you need some more time off?" he asked, over his head.

"That's the last thing I need. My job is all I have right now. I don't need more time to worry about me. I can just work and keep moving forward. If you don't mind, it's the start of my weekend, so I'm going home, drink some wine, and watch some bad TV shows."

• • •

Gin loaded the radio app on her phone and queued up the 90s music station she had created. As soon as she heard the first line of "What is Love," she tapped the button to move on to the next song. This time it came up with Natalie Merchant.

"Much better," she said, setting the phone down on the vanity next to a string of candles she'd lit.

She shrugged off her robe, leaving it in a pile on the bathroom floor. Curls of steam rose from the tub. The skylight above it was opaque from the moisture. She dipped an exploratory toe into the water before easing into the hot bath. The enveloping heat was soothing.

Over on the vanity, a nearly empty bottle of red wine sat next to a glass that was half full. She cupped the glass in one hand and brought it to her lips. In one quick motion, she downed the rest of the glass and tried to set it down next to the tub. The glass slipped from between her wet fingers and shattered on the tile floor. She peered over the edge, frowning at the mess.

"Whatever," she mumbled and reached for the bottle. It was just out of reach. After stretching her arm as far as she could and failing miserably, she gave up with sigh.

Gin's eyelids were heavy. The grueling week had taken

its toll on her both physically and emotionally. She did her best to just focus on her breathing, clearing the clutter from her mind. Breathe in. Breathe out.

A grunge band carried on the background – maybe Nirvana? She reached over and tapped the button to stop the music. Breathe in. Breathe out. Breathe in. Breathe out.

Out of the stillness came something that sounded less like a whisper and more like someone exhaling. She forced her eyes open, checking the room without turning her head. The bathroom was washed in the warm light of her candles. The flickering lights reflected off the mirror and danced around the ceiling.

She heard it again – louder this time. Someone said her name. Her eyes darted around the room. The door was still closed. The linen closet was closed. No one was there.

Virginia…

She looked up at the skylight. A pale face stared at her through the steamy window. She sat up straight, never taking her eyes off the face.

Do it, Virginia…

"Do what?" she found herself asking, mesmerized by the figure.

One quick slice…

She looked over the edge of the tub. The shards of broken glass were scattered all over the floor.

Yes…

Gin watched in horror as she reached out for the nearest piece. She wanted to pull the hand back, but couldn't. Her fingers wrapped around the sliver and squeezed. A warm trail of blood rolled down her arm as she raised the glass above the tub.

Join us…

Her hand shook sending a rain of crimson droplets across the surface of the water. She touched the jagged edge of the glass to her other wrist. It would all be over soon – a little more pressure to make all the pain go away.

She stared back at the grinning visage in the skylight. Something was deeply wrong. She assumed it was a trick of the light at first, an image shaped by shadows and steam, but it wasn't. The thing had two deep-set black orbs for eyes.

She hurled the glass shard across the room. "NO!"

The thing above hissed and vanished.

Rising out the tub, she grabbed her robe from the floor and shook out the pieces of glass. She covered the broken shards with a plush towel and carefully made her way to the sink. The cold water bit at the cuts on her hand, but it helped to clear her head. She grabbed a small towel and wound it around her hand to staunch the bleeding. She needed stitches, but not right now.

As Gin raced to her bedroom, she could hear someone knocking on the door downstairs. The slow beats were monotonous, but spaced farther apart than a normal knock. She hastily pulled on a t-shirt and sweatpants. The last thing she grabbed on the way back into the hall was her pistol. The Glock felt reassuring in her hand.

The knocking continued as she descended the stairs. When she reached the foyer, she could hear the voices outside. They were empty, lacking emotion, and she could almost feel the words as well as hear them.

"Please let us in," one said.

"We need to use your phone," another demanded.

Gin peered through the peephole. Three figures stood on her doorstep. All three were dressed in dark clothes.

There were two teenage boys, one tall and one short, and a little girl standing behind them. Their sharp features glowed in the moonlight. The short boy was closest to the door and continued to knock. She could feel his unblinking black eyes staring at her through the door.

"I'm cold. Can we can come in?" the little girl asked.

Gin thumbed off the safety on her gun. "What did you do to Maya?"

The knocking stopped.

"It was her time," the tall one said in his grating monotone.

"Past her time," the little girl said.

Gin unlocked the deadbolt, took a deep breath, and pulled open door. The temperature in the room dropped immediately. With her courage waning, she leveled the gun at the mysterious figures. "I don't understand. What do you mean it was past her time?"

"We need to come in. We won't hurt you," the short one said.

"Answer. The. Question."

The little girl stepped forward. "She eluded her fate."

"Like you," the tall one added.

Tears welled up in her eyes. "Like me?" she mouthed. Her legs quivered and gave out, sending Gin to her knees. The gun slipped from her fingers. Hard sobs escaped her lips as she tried to process what she'd just heard.

"I'm sorry Joel. I'm so sorry. I miss you so much."

"Don't be afraid," the three said in unison.

"I love you, Joel. I always will. I promise."

"Let us in," they chanted in their monotone. "Let us in."

"No! You can't come in. Go away. I was wrong. I want to live. Do you hear me? I want to live!"

The cold air swirled around her. She squeezed her eyes together tightly, sat back, and pulled her knees up to her chest. The monotone voices turned into whispers. The breathless words were coming from all over; circling around her in little eddies.

"I want to live!"

The whispers gave way to the beating of wings.

Gin opened her eyes to see a trio of ravens, their dark eyes studying her, looping and diving around her before finally flying off into the night sky.

"I want to live."

The Door

BY JOE POWERS

Cellars are often scary places. There's just something about them that hits on a subconscious level turning the mind to musty, dusty corners where shadows lurk and unseen things seek refuge, only darting about at the corners of the eye and on the fringe of the imagination's darker areas.

Bruce Lowry had a very vivid imagination and did not care for such places at all as a general rule, but was less reserved than he normally would have been due to an unusual feature of the one he was currently standing in.

It was a cellar not unlike many others: damp and chilly, dimly lit by a single bare light bulb and generously coated with dust and thick cobwebs. In this unpleasant setting the unlikely pair of virtual strangers stood, looking the door over carefully. It was set into a recess in the back wall of the cellar, made of heavy wood - oak possibly, though with the dense layer of dust it was difficult to be sure—and held together with solid-looking wrought iron bands and heavy bolts secured with thick washers. Bruce traced one finger along the edge of the frame, admiring the elaborate craftsmanship. The door filled the space of the doorway perfectly, without so much as a crack or seam on either side, above or below. This, despite the fact it was set into a stone wall into which the hole was chiseled by hand over a century ago. Old-world craftsmanship; a lost art today, he thought. On either side of the door a pair of large iron rings were set into the stone. Four more identical rings were affixed into the great door—top, bottom and either side—and interlaced through all of them was a thick steel chain, drawn taut and clasped together by a huge, square padlock.

"There, you've seen it," said his companion, a thin, bespectacled woman with wispy, graying hair and an un-smiling face. Her name was Nancy Hollister, formerly his great uncle's lawyer and now the executor of his estate. She bore the look of someone who would normally never set foot in such a dismal place as she now found herself, and who was utterly disgusted at the prospect of remaining one second longer than necessary. She had a nasal, piercing voice and spoke in a clipped manner. "And now, you'd be well advised to forget all about it."

Bruce was trying his best to be polite, though he found her to be rather unpleasant. "Forget about it? Why, what's in there? And why's it locked down so tight?" He'd been miffed to learn a condition of ownership of the old house was that entry into whatever lay behind the door was strictly forbidden, and by the idea that he should have to adhere to such a ridiculous rule. He had hoped for at least a bit of background from the tight-lipped lawyer, but nothing pertinent appeared to be forthcoming.

"To the best of my knowledge it was originally a wine cellar," she replied, waving her hand absently at an unseen cobweb in front of her face. "As for why it's locked, I have no idea, not that it matters in the least for our purposes. It's immaterial. All I know is that the original owner of the house took great pains to seal this doorway and to ensure it remained so. You will become the fifth owner hence, and in all those years and through every exchange of hands, the door has remained sealed. I am given to understand the previous owner, one Charles Lowry – your great uncle - went so far as to keep the door at the top of the stairs locked as well. Indeed, I have it on good authority that Mr. Lowry did not one time set foot in this cellar, beyond his initial inspection, in the twenty seven years during which he resided here."

"Twenty seven years," Bruce repeated softly. "We're the first people to set foot down here in almost three decades?"

He glanced around at the dingy surroundings and guessed he could believe that based on the dusty conditions. He turned to the lawyer in amazement. "How in the world could any man last so long without his curiosity getting the better of him even once?"

"I cannot speak for the elder Mr. Lowry, sir, nor for any of his predecessors. As for myself, I believe I could be persuaded to redirect my attention from an object—regardless of the appeal - if I had reason to believe it was in my best interests to do so."

Bruce considered her words carefully. What could she be referring to? Why would it be in her, or anyone's, best interests to stay out of there? What could possibly be back there worth sealing up for over a century? His inquisitive nature swirled out of control. The urge to have a look was strong, but for the moment it seemed it was out of the question. They finished with the inspection of the cellar, and as they headed back upstairs he managed a weak smile and did his best to endure the rest of tour.

By the time the paperwork had been finalized and his uncle's lawyer had taken her leave, Bruce convinced himself it would be foolhardy to deprive himself of at least a look behind the door. The terms of the will had been clear, but who would ever know? "Just a quick peek, for posterity," he rationalized. "If I don't see anything interesting, I'll seal it back up and forget about it." Thus persuaded, he set about searching for the key to the lock. Both chain and lock were too thick for bolt cutters or any other such method. He'd been told the key was hidden in the house somewhere, and made a mental note to have a look around. If it proved too difficult to locate he would bring in a locksmith, but very discreetly and only as a last resort.

He recalled the offhanded way the lawyer had described the specifics of the will, how there had been next to no money as part of the estate. When Bruce had asked how anybody could afford to own and keep up such a house as this with no money to his name, she had replied simply "I didn't say he had no money, Mr. Lowry. Only that he left none on the books when he passed." Her cryptic words had implied there was a fortune, just none that anybody had been able to discover.

The key was, as it turned out, not in the least difficult to locate - it hung from a thin chain on a peg in the wall opposite the door, not ten paces distant. He traced his finger along its length, curious as to how anyone could ignore the impulse to unlock the door, especially with the means to do so dangling so prominently and tantalizingly at hand. He slipped it from the peg and walked back toward the door, the chain dangling between his fingers.

He hefted the lock which, encumbered as it was by the weight of the chain, was considerably heavy. He stared down at it, on the verge of the point of no return, but suddenly froze, his head cocked quizzically to one side. He thought he'd heard a faint rasping sound, which seemed to come from directly in front of him—on the other side of the door. He listened intently, but heard nothing. "Had to be an echo from one of the chain links hitting the door," he reasoned. He eased the key into the hole and paused again—certain he had heard another sound through the door. While the rational portion of his mind told him there had been no sound, he strained to catch any hint of the noise that had tweaked his attention. For a moment he had the distinct sensation of something pressed heavily against the opposite side of the door, maybe six inches of wood and iron separating him from whatever it was, holding its breath. Of course there could be nothing in there, he knew. But still, the hairs on his body stood on end; the room pulsed with a palpable sense of eager anticipation.

He briefly considered the possibility that those before him had a legitimate reason for keeping such a vigilant guard over the door. It made sense that over that many years someone would have broken the seal at some point, unless there was something extremely convincing preventing it. Superstition would have played into it for sure, and probably whatever story had been handed down from each man's predecessor, but would that really be enough to sustain the pattern over such a prolonged period?

"This is ridiculous," he muttered. "How could anything be alive back there? After a hundred years, whatever it is would be awfully hungry." He shook his head with a nervous laugh, then jumped at the sudden sound despite his reassurances. His heart was racing, and he scolded himself for letting his imagination run away with him. Drawing a long, slow breath he shoved the key into the lock. It slid far more easily than he would have expected from such an old and obviously neglected device. There was a dull metallic clink as the head struck the back. He gave it a tentative twist and heard a sharp ping, followed by a click as the lock fell open. Through the door he imagined he heard a quick intake of breath.

He wiped the back of one hand across his eyes, and though the temperature was a good ten degrees cooler in the cellar than in the house above, he found he was sweating profusely. Last chance, a voice in his head said. It's not too late yet. Push that lock shut again, go upstairs, and forget about this. For a moment he very nearly did just that. The energy in the room pulsed like a live wire, seeming to hum at a barely audible level. The anticipation of what lay beyond the door was palpable.

"To hell with it," he said aloud, and lifted the lock from the chain, dropping it to the stone floor.

The metallic clank made him jump, and he realized he was on the verge of panic. If I don't keep going, I'll never be at peace, he thought. He took a deep breath and unthreaded the heavy chain from the rings. The chain must have weighed nearly a hundred pounds, and he was winded by the time he'd set it on the floor beside the lock. Despite the effort he realized he was placing it as gently as he could, doing his best to be as quiet as possible in the process.

Something in the back of his mind stopped him once again. He felt he owed it to himself to explore the sensation, however briefly, and either put his mind at ease or turn away from the door forever. His mind swirled with possibilities. The imaginative part of his mind fairly screamed at him to put this nonsense behind him and forget about it. His logical, inquisitive part insisted there had to be a reason behind all the secrecy.

Ultimately, as inexplicably, irrationally frightened as he was, he knew in his heart there was no way he could force himself to ignore the door. Regardless of what may befall him as a result from his urges—however impossibly ridiculous—he had come too far to turn back. It would haunt him constantly, and it was only a matter of time before he was drawn to the door again, whatever the consequences.

He placed his trembling hand on the handle and gripped it tightly, trying to steady his nerves. He took another deep breath, let it out slowly, and pulled. The door swung much more easily than he had expected, as if a great force were pushing from the other side. Off balance, he stumbled back a step. There was an audible puff of stale air, and he caught a fleeting glimpse of the interminable darkness which lay beyond.

His curiosity was soon satisfied and he quickly realized both his predictions had been right. There was nothing alive behind the door. And it was very hungry.

Regular, Normal People

BY GRANT JERKINS

Religion is a funny thing. We've all got a little bit of it inside us. Even if you say you don't believe in God or Jesus or Zeus or Pan. There are no atheists in foxholes. That's a very true statement. If your child is in ICU after getting run over by a car, or you're waiting for the biopsy results from the lump on your left testicle, or you're hunkered down in your basement while a tornado barrels right through the middle of your neighborhood—you pray. If you believe in God and Jesus, then you direct your prayers straight to them. If you've maybe fallen away from Christianity and have started thinking Jesus is just a made-up story, well, when the shit hits the fan—or when the tumor hits your balls—you're gonna revert right back to believing. You're going to grasp at straws. And if you're maybe one of those people who never believed in a damn thing, never believed in anything supernatural at all, well, when the doctors tell you that your little boy might end up brain dead if they can't get the intracranial pressure to go down, then I submit that you will fall to your knees and pray and beg and beseech whatever power might be out there to please, please, please intervene and save your child.

There are no atheists in foxholes. Everybody believes

(or at least hopes) in something beyond themselves when they're alone in the dark with no chance to escape.

We are regular, normal people. We live in the suburbs. There is nothing special about us.

I guess me and Jennie were about on the same page religion-wise when we got married. Christians. That's the way we both were raised, but we didn't go to church much (at all) or even say grace before meals. But we believed, more or less. Neither one of us wanted to go to Hell. We accepted that Jesus Christ was the path to heaven.

I understand now why cultures frown on people from different religions getting married. When you're young and in love, that stuff seems insignificant. But when you're older and not-as-in-love, and you can see death as a real eventuality, your life moves in a more spiritual direction. That's when those differences can start to show, to put a strain on a marriage. That's the way it was with me and Jennie. She started believing more and more, and I started believing less and less.

It's like echoes that get stronger instead of weaker. When we first got married, I only drank on the weekends. Maybe a six pack on Friday and Saturday night. Then pretty soon I started wanting a beer or two after I got home from Overstock World on weeknights, to unwind. It just got to be more and more, and after a while, I switched to vodka because it was a lot cheaper than beer. More bang for your buck. Vodka and grapefruit juice. That's what I drank seven nights a week. I'd sit up late at night and play Spades on the computer with other people online and my Internet name that I gave myself was *Vodkaniac*.

Do you see the echo? How it got stronger? How I started out just having some beer on the weekends and ended up as Vodkaniac as the echo got stronger? That's like what happened with Jennie and the religion stuff.

A girlfriend invited her to church one Sunday. And she liked it well enough I guess. A social thing more than anything else.

Then it just got to be more and more. Like how I was drinking more and more.

She started saying grace over our meals. Which was nice. That reminded me of being a kid and how my father always mumbled a little something up to God before we ate the dinner my mother had prepared.

But it got where she would say weird things, too. Like if we got in an argument about me drinking too much, she would say, "I plead the blood of the lamb," and just walk away. I didn't even know what that meant. Still don't.

If anything good happened, she would say God had made it happen. Like if we were real far behind on the bills, close to getting our electricity shut off or something, and I worked two extra overnight shifts and brought home a check that was fat with overtime, she would say, God had really blessed us.

I would say, no, he did not. I blessed us. I'm the one who put in all those hours under fluorescent lights, setting up endcaps and in-store displays. She would say that God took care of all our needs, and He made that overtime available and kept me healthy enough to work it. That she had prayed and asked Him to get all our bills paid, and He had answered her prayers.

That made me really mad. For one thing, it just completely took my free will out of the equation, like I was just some kind of zombie being controlled by God. So even though I did all the work, God got all the credit. Jennie got some credit too, because she was the one who had prayed and asked God to provide for our needs. I did all the work, and God and Jennie took all the credit.

She started at a new church. Fundamentalist. Charismatic. It was called Church of God of Prophecy, and it plain scared me. She drug me in there one time. The preacher got up on stage and started talking in tongues. It was just gibberish. It wasn't any language; it was just something he was making up on the spot. He walked back and forth, holding his belly and laughing. It wasn't like real laughing, he was going, "Ho! Ho! Ho!—Ho! Ho! Ho!" over and over again. Jennie knew I was greatly disturbed. She leaned over and told me he was "laughing in the spirit." Said it was joy that was supernaturally given.

Those people weren't but one step away from snake handling, and I didn't want a goddamn thing to do with them.

It seemed like the harder she believed, the more I questioned it.

There was a bad tornado up in Alabama, ripped right through a residential neighborhood. All the houses on one side of the street were completely destroyed, flattened like a giant had stepped on them. On the other side of the street, all the houses were fine, not even a loose shutter or shingle blown off the roof. It was just one of those freakish weather things you hear about sometimes. We watched while they interviewed the people on CNN, and this woman whose house was spared talked about how it sounded like a freight train tearing through the neighborhood. She said her house was groaning and shaking, and they were all hunkered down in the basement, and just praying, praying to God to save them, to spare her and her family.

And He did. Their home stood through the storm. Not a speck of damage.

Jennie turned to me and said that proved the existence of God. If you worshiped Him and acknowledged Him, then He would acknowledge you in your time of need. But if you turned your back on Him, then He would turn His back on you.

And all I could think was, well what about all them people on the other side of the street? They weren't praying? None of them believed in God? That was just crazy. But I didn't speak up, because I'd learned to keep my mouth shut. No matter what kind of logic I tried to use, there was always a reason, even if that reason was *we'll never understand the mind of God.*

One time, I told her I just didn't understand the concept of hell. That if I had a child, and I needed to punish that child, I wouldn't shove him in a furnace and burn him to death for ten million years. Why would God do that to us if we were his children? It just didn't make sense.

Jennie said I was beset by demons that were clouding my mind, and she started in on how God had sacrificed his only begotten son, so that we could have forgiveness and cleansing of our sins. It was my choice to turn my back on salvation when Jesus had showed me the way. But you know, that still didn't answer my question about a parent shoving his child in a furnace. Sounded to me like God was one evil motherfucker.

She had this mole on her thigh, and it started looking weird. The mole was kind of bubbly, like road tar on a hot day. She didn't want to go to the doctor, said she would pray for divine healing. I said okay, but I went to the computer and looked up skin cancer on the Internet. Looked at pictures. There wasn't any doubt in my mind that the mole on Jennie's thigh was cancer. Melanoma. And melanoma is the worst kind of skin cancer you can get. It spreads.

I told her what I found out. That I was pretty sure she had melanoma, but she said God was going to heal her, He was going to deliver her of it. I told her that I didn't think that was the way God worked. I said, if you're standing on train tracks, and a train is coming straight at you, you don't close your eyes and ask God to make the train disappear. You step off the tracks. And if you've got cancer on your thigh, you don't pray it away; you go to the fucking doctor.

She wouldn't do it. I started getting myself used to the idea of living as a widower, because I knew that's how this was all going to end up. But do you know what happened? That spot on her thigh just kind of started drying up. It turned brownish red and got real flaky and powdery. And then, after about a week, it scabbed over and fell off. Like it was never there. Now, you tell me, did God do that? I sure don't know. Maybe He did.

Jennie ended up getting pregnant. Which was kind of a miracle in itself, because we didn't hardly ever have sex anymore, mostly because I was usually too drunk to perform in that capacity. Sometimes I think me and Jennie both have a hole inside of us, and I'm trying to fill my hole up with alcohol, and she's trying to fill hers up with God. What neither one of us knew was that hole can't ever be filled up.

When we found out she was expecting, I did slow down on my drinking, and Jennie pulled back on her religion. I wanted to be a good father. We had been trying to have a family for a long time, but Jennie just couldn't ever get pregnant. We're just normal, regular people, so we didn't have money to pay for fertility treatments or artificial insemination or anything like that. Time went by and we kind of gave up trying; I started drinking and she started testifying. I guess probably not having a child was a big part of that hole we were trying to fill up.

So of course she said God had answered her prayers and knocked her up, but I could notice a kind of calming of the religious mania, and I'm sure she noticed I switched from vodka back to beer. Things seemed like they were getting better for us. The echoes were dying out instead of getting stronger.

Jennie l ooked like someone had planted a watermelon seed in her belly and it grew. She was beautiful.

There were some problems with the pregnancy. She got gestational diabetes and I had to give her insulin shots or else the baby would get too big inside her. That got her scared that she might lose the baby or it would end up being born retarded or something. She turned to The Lord for help and got back in with that church.

They held a healing service for her. I went. How could I not go? It was my wife and my baby.

The congregation all prayed for her while the preacher brought her up to the little pulpit, laid hands on her and commanded the demon that had sickened her womb and threatened her child to be expelled in the name and the everlasting power of the living God, Jesus Christ. Then he got down on his knees and started that laughing in the spirit. "Ho! Ho! Ho!—Ho! Ho! Ho!" Over and over again right into Jennie's privates. I thought about my little unborn child in there feeling those sound waves washing over it.

The preacher reached under the podium and brought

out a plain pine box with a screen lid. He opened it up and brought out two snakes, looked like copperheads to me. At first I thought he was going to put one on Jennie, but she was already walking back to our pew. The preacher held the snakes up over his head, and let them crawl up his arm, over his shoulders and around his neck. He would pick one off his body, and let it crawl back up his arm again, all the time just bellowing how this church was filled with the loving spirit of the lord Jesus Christ, and how his belief in the Lord would keep the poisonous serpents from biting him.

I wanted a drink.

Since I had gone to the church with her, Jennie agreed to keep going to the doctor, too. That's what marriage is. Compromise. She said that she had been divinely delivered and given a supernatural healing. She knew that the baby was fine, but she would go back to the doctor for me, for my peace of mind.

After her last appointment, she said the doctor told her that they couldn't detect a fetal heartbeat. They did an ultrasound and that confirmed it. The baby had died inside of her. They told her that they could put her in the hospital and chemically induce labor, or she could continue to carry it and let it come out naturally on its own. She would give birth to a dead baby.

The news shook me up pretty bad. I knew if it was me, I'd go to the hospital and let them get it out of me. I couldn't walk around day after day knowing I was carrying a dead child inside of me. I didn't even know if I could stand to stay in the house with her, knowing she had that dead thing in her womb. It broke my heart, but I told her that.

She had this wild look in her eyes and laughed at me the way an adult laughs at a child who says something naïve and cute. She said those tests didn't confirm anything. That they were wrong, and if somehow they were right, that her child really had died inside her, then God would bring her baby back to life.

We waited to see if God was going to bless us with a miracle and our baby was going to be born happy and healthy, or if Jennie would spontaneously abort the poor dead thing.

I set up camp on the couch. I couldn't sleep in the bedroom with her. I'm sorry, but I couldn't. She was on her own.

The preacher from the Church of God of Prophecy made a housecall. He stayed in there with her for three hours, and I could hear him speaking in tongues. I could hear that Santa Claus chortle. Laughing in the spirit. After he left, I looked in on her, and I saw in the corner that the preacher had left his pine box behind. The one with the screen top. To let in air.

The baby came in the night. It was born dead just like the doctor said. She won't let me take it away from her, said Jesus was going to heal our child, and that I had demons in me, and that I had to rebuke those demons so that our child could live.

At some point, I'm going to have to call somebody to come get her out of there. The fire department, maybe. I don't know.

We are regular, normal people. You need to understand that. We live in the suburbs. There is nothing special about us.

She's in there now—with those copperheads crawling

all over her, holding our dead baby, and laughing in the spirit.

I'm gonna go out and get me a bottle of vodka. And pray.

The Hungry Ones

BY JOHN LEAHY

The water was very cold, but didn't bother them much. They worked their way up along the coast, catching some incredible waves on the way while a shade-wearing Maurice watched them from the shore, leaning up against the front of the four-by-four, smiling and stoned. The further north they progressed the quieter the locations became, and by the time they entered the wilderness of the Northern Cape, they practically had the beaches, bays and coves to themselves.

They paid little heed to the rapid deterioration of the road beneath them as they were too preoccupied with the captivating natural sights all around them. Steenboks prancing along the veld, male oryx butting each other, seals basking on beaches while over them cormorants swept onto the truculent Atlantic and dived beneath its surface for food, while others, post-dive and their appetites sated, stood on rocks, their wings open wide in the sun. The wild flowers of Namaqualand were particularly breathtaking as they found themselves driving through a smorgasbord of color: a gigantic, living patchwork quilt making the most of the South African spring.

After surfing a cracking reef break at Port Nolloth, they set out on the last stage of their northbound crusade toward Alexander Bay at the mouth of the Orange river. There they would say goodbye to Maurice as he continued on into Namibia and they returned to Cape Town. The road for this final stretch of their adventure was little more than a bumpy dirt-track and proved laborious. The area was also pretty desolate. An hour into the journey they hadn't come across a single person or dwelling. The surf looked enticing, but with this section of the coastline being so rugged, crag-strewn and kelp-infested, there was nowhere worth stopping to break the monotony of the journey.

Eventually they came across a promising spot: a tiny bay with low, sheer cliffs at both sides and big, regular, seaweed-free barrels. Pete pulled off of the "road" and onto the grassy verge before descending a gentle slope toward the sand. At the base of the slope they alighted onto a ribbon of stones. As they shuddered their way over this, Wayne observed the caves in the cliffs: one in each, high, wide, dark holes boring into the rock.

The four-by-four skipped onto the firm, wet sand and the moment Pete killed the engine his phone rang. He took the call.

"Hey Frank" he smiled.

Emma and Wayne grinned at each other. Frank was Pete's younger brother and a good weekend hell-raiser. He'd called his older sibling every Sunday since the beginning of their trip. Wayne looked at his watch. It was one pm, which meant Frank was probably shambling out of a party or nightclub somewhere in the greater Los Angeles area. Leaving Pete to his "conversation", Emma and Wayne got out and went around to the back of the four-by-four. While they changed into their wetsuits Maurice gazed out at the ocean, the frolics of what sounded like an Irish jig tooting from his tin whistle.

"What's that one called?" Emma asked him as Wayne took their boards down from the roof-rack.

"One I just came up with myself, actually" Maurice answered. "Must work on it. I think I'll call it...*Surfer's Fancy*."

"It's nice" Emma said.

Maurice nodded his gratitude. "Thanks" he said.

"Keep playing it" Wayne said, handing Emma her board.

Maurice began playing again and they passed by him, headed for the water. As they went by the front of the four-by-four Emma waved at Pete who was still inside on the phone. He waved back. Wayne gave him a sympathetic thumbs-up and Pete rolled his eyes in amused exasperation, shaking his head a little.

Emma and Wayne strode quickly toward the ocean, the sound of the crashing waves amplifying as the lilt of *Surfer's Fancy* began to wane. The waves were big, Wayne guessing their height at around the twelve foot mark. Nice and long and clean. This would be good.

He gave a look at the cave to his left, which was still slightly ahead of them. There was a small flash in his stomach and he slowed to a stop, staring at the cave-mouth, blinking. Emma turned and looked at him.

"Wayne?" she asked. "What's up?"

He didn't answer immediately, still gazing at the cave-mouth. He blinked.

"Nothing" he said eventually, looking away from the dark orifice. "Just...thought I saw something."

"What did you see?" Emma asked, turning toward the

cave.

"Ah!" he said dismissively. "Nothing. Too much weed last night I guess."

"Race you!" Emma said. She turned and bolted for the water. Wayne remained rooted where he was, distracted. He looked at the cave-mouth again. Whatever he'd seen, or thought he'd seen, a moment earlier was there no longer. All was now as it should be, the blue-black rock surrounding the dark void in the cliff gazing timelessly back at him, perfectly normal.

No long, shiny, black segmented stick-like thing protruding from the gloom...

"WAYNE!"

Snapped from his reverie, Wayne saw Emma ahead of him, a slightly puzzled half-smile on her features. He began jogging toward her.

"Sorry" he said sheepishly.

"Come on!" she said when he was nearly level with her, and began galloping toward the water again. He took off after her. *Fuck* Maurice and his high-grade Moroccan. Wayne had obviously done way too much of it last night with the fucker and was paying the price for it today. He'd been woozy up until noon and now he was hallucinating –.

To clear his thoughts he let his eyes drop to Emma's rear up ahead of him. An impressive piece, it looked incredible in a wetsuit. He'd had it in his hands and in his bed a few times, before she and Pete hooked up. A pang of sorrow darted through him. It happened every now and then as he experienced fleeting moments of regret at not having made something more permanent with her. Too late now, though. Now she was a one-man woman, she and Pete being very much in love.

He picked up his pace and drew level with her. Their boards hit the shallows more or less in sync and they began paddling out. A minute later Wayne was in his first tube, all thoughts of strange black sticks, missed opportunities with Emma and head-wrecking weed gone from his mind. When he made his exit Emma cheered him from nearby and he threw his arms in the air in triumph. It had been a perfect ride all right.

Emma caught some serious waves herself. After watching her tame a particularly impressive beast Wayne gave a glance at the shore. No longer playing his whistle, Maurice was puffing a joint. Pete was still on the phone in the four-by-four.

Feeling brave, Wayne chanced a fearsome-looking fifteen-footer, but catching it all wrong fell at the worst possible time. The elephantine lip mercilessly bullied him like a rag doll all the way down to the sea-bed where he twisted his right arm upon impact with some coral.

His ascent toward the surface was torturous, each propelling stroke of his injured arm causing a horrific flash of pain from elbow to shoulder. Relief rushed through him when he felt Emma's arm clasp around him. When they broke the surface he told her what happened and she helped him sit onto his board. She asked him if he thought he could paddle in and Wayne said he thought he'd manage it. They got moving. Each stroke of his right arm was extremely painful for Wayne, he squinted and gritted his teeth each time he had to use it. They were almost in the shallows when Wayne became suddenly aware that Emma was not by his side. He looked behind him and a knot tightened in his gut. Emma was inert on her board, staring unblinking straight ahead, her eyes a mixture of fear and utter disbelief.

Following her line of sight Wayne saw a monstrous, multi-legged ink-black form—*THERE'S your black stick*—something that he could only describe as a giant spider, standing motionless outside the cave to his left. At the back of the four-by-four stood Pete, holding his surfboard, gazing incrtly at the creature by the cliff. Wayne could just make out the strains of *Surfer's Fancy* as Maurice, facing the ocean and oblivious to the shocking new arrival, played his tin whistle at the other side of the vehicle.

What happened next took place in seconds.

The spider-thing flashed forward.

"PETE!" Emma screamed as her boyfriend dropped his board and lunged for the back door of the four-by-four.

The speed of the abomination hurtling toward Pete was terrifying to witness as Wayne watched it literally *streak* across the sand. It covered the seventy meters or so between its former position and Pete in little over a second. Pete had his hand on the door-handle when the horror collided with him, smashing him against the back door with such violence that the vehicle rocked visibly.

"PEEEEEETE!!!" Emma shrieked in desperate terror.

Pete slumped to the sand on his front. The spider stood over him, its huge, unspeakablc lcgs, not far off the height of the four-by-four's roof, on either side of Pete's prone form. Wayne could make out some faint movement in his friend's downed figure, Pete's arms and right leg striving weakly to drag himself somewhere. More animated movement caught Wayne's eye and he saw Maurice arrive around the driver's side and freeze, having arrived just in time to witness the nightmare's mouth begin taking bites out of the back of Pete's wetsuit.

"STAWWWWP!!!" Emma wailed, sobbing. "GET AWAY FROM HIM! STAAAWP!!!"

Wayne saw Maurice look to his left, do a double-take and grab the handle of the driver's door. He just had the door closed behind him when another spider, smaller than the first, crashed against it, blasting Maurice across to the passenger side. The wheels on the driver's side lifted into the air and the four-by-four tilted over on its side. The spider ran at it again, this time colliding with its exposed undercarriage and forcing the vehicle onto its roof, upside down. Two of its front legs stabbed against the passenger window now, smashing the glass and reaching inside. There was a loud BANG and the spider frantically withdrew from the vehicle, the last three feet or so of one of its probing legs hanging loosely, almost severed from the remainder of the appendage.

There was a horrible, guttural, KEK! KEK! KEK! as the terror flinched warily backward from the four-by-four. It kept up its repetition of the KEK! sound, which Wayne's close to horror-overloaded brain presumed was an expression of pain. Numbly he realised that Maurice had had the presence of mind to liberate the gun they'd bought for protection from its pocket beneath the armrest and used it.

Emma was wading ashore in the shallows, still screaming and crying at the big spider to get away from her boyfriend, to leave him alone. The back of the now unmoving Pete's swimsuit was gone, the flesh it had covered now a ragged mush as the spider dined on it. Suddenly the spider's head flicked to the left and Wayne saw something long and reddish-white go flying from its mouth.

Pete's spinal chord.

"PETE!" Emma bawled from up ahead of Wayne, her voice more laden with despair now than panic as she watched the devouring of her lover.

Movement caught the corner of Wayne's eye and his heart, which was already hammering full pelt in his chest, began to race even faster. Another huge spider, as big as the one feasting on Pete, was standing outside the cave where Wayne had seen his first *hallucination*. It was facing the water, or more accurately, the people *in* the water. Wayne's head flashed back toward Emma, who had reached the shore.

"Get back in the water Emma!" he shouted instinctively.

"NO-O-O-O PEEEEEETE!" Emma lamented as though she hadn't heard him.

The spider bolted toward her.

"EMMA!"

She began to turn toward Wayne and seeing the beast galloping toward her, ran back into the water, screaming. The arrival of the demon was dreadful, the pounding of its legs on the sand sounding like some terrible, many-legged horse. It exploded into the water after her, almost getting her, but pulled back quickly, unwilling to pursue her deeper into the shallows. It reversed to the water's edge, where it stood, motionless.

Crying and sobbing, Emma hauled herself onto a seated position on her board beside Wayne. She regarded the terrible form on the shore for a few seconds then turned to Wayne.

"What the hell ARE they, Wayne?" she asked in a bewildered, hopeless tone.

"I don't know" Wayne replied.

The awful giant on the shoreline remained where it was, silent and unmoving.

• • •

There was a tear in the thigh of her wetsuit where one of the monster's pointed legs had slashed her, leaving a deep gash in the flesh beneath. She had to keep a hand pressed down hard on the wound to stem the bleeding. A thick worm of worry uncoiled in Wayne's gut as he regarded the faint red trail in the water. The South African coast was notorious for sharks.

The smaller spider trotted down to the waterline where it joined Emma and Wayne's jailer in its vigil. The two creatures kept watch over the prisoners until the big one decided to turn on its companion. The ensuing skirmish ended with the big one tearing off the hanging-loose part of the small one's injured leg and eating it while the maimed victim hopped and jittered about on the sand. When its brief meal was complete, the big one ambled back up the beach toward the four-by-four. Wayne could just make out Maurice squatted in the back of it, holding the gun in both hands. When the big one arrived by the vehicle it smashed its way in through the back window, reaching for Maurice.

"OH GOD!" Emma cried as Maurice darted away from the probing pincers, pressing himself up against the opposite door. A gunshot rang out and the spider flinched. The other big spider, picking through the almost skeletal remains of Pete saw a chance for a second meal and crashed through the window at Maurice's back.

The gun went off as a screaming Maurice was dragged out onto the sand where the spider promptly silenced him by tearing away most of the man's neck, almost decapitating him.

"OH NO-O-O-O-O!!!" Emma wailed.

The other big spider, outraged at the devious theft, raced around the four-by-four and launched an assault on the dinner-stealer. The thief was quickly bested and moved off in the direction of its cave while the victor enjoyed its meal. Emma cried softly beside Wayne while the small spider scavenged at the remains of her boyfriend.

• • •

Wayne looked at his watch, his arm shaking before him. He was freezing. It was five-thirty. They'd been in the water for four and a half hours.

"We have to go."

Wayne looked sideways. Emma was staring at the shoreline where the three spiders were standing in a line, facing them, waiting.

"What do you mean, 'go'?" Wayne asked. "Go where?"

"Out of the bay. Head north or south. Try and come ashore somewhere."

"With THAT?" Wayne asked, looking at her cut leg. "Are you crazy?"

She looked at him. "Can you paddle?"

He stared at her, blinking. She was resolute, he could see, decided. He sighed and stroked the water with his right hand. He almost yelped in pain.

"Christ!" he said through gritted teeth. "Not a chance."

She moved closer to him. "I'll get help and come back, ok?"

He said nothing for a moment. "Head north" he eventually said. "Might have a better chance of meeting someone."

They embraced. "Take care, ok?" he said over the lump in his throat.

"You too" she said.

He watched her paddle over the waves and disappear around the northern cliff, leaving him alone with the spiders.

• • •

One by one, they left.

It was growing dark when the smaller one, (the only one who hadn't had a proper meal), headed off toward its cave. If he hadn't already urinated a few minutes before, Wayne would have flooded his wetsuit with relief at the sight of the spider disappearing into the hole in the rock. He waited another half hour before he headed toward the shore. When he got off of his board in the shallows he collapsed in the water, his frozen feet useless.

He crawled onto the sand, his entire body shivering. The air was icy, the South African sky open to the stars. His teeth chattering uncontrollably, he headed for the four-by-four, looking from cliff to cliff for any sign of the monsters. He wondered about Emma. Had she made it ashore? Was she walking some bleak road right now, blue with the cold? Maybe she was warm in a jeep, headed toward him with a band of rescuers. This last thought gave him a fleeting lift which was quickly cancelled by his arrival at the four-by-four. Trying not to look at the midden that had once been Maurice he picked up the gun at its side. He heard what sounded like a twig breaking. He turned behind him to his left.

The small spider (it was still more than half the height

of the four-by-four) was standing a couple of meters away, motionless, one shortened leg at odds with its seven hideous others.

Wayne raised his quivering, gun-holding arm and pointed the weapon at the nightmare. He pulled the trigger.

Click.

Empty.

Then the terror was upon him, ripping him open. He opened his mouth to cry out before he went but his scream never left his frozen throat.

Parts

BY JACQUELINE SEEWALD

"Your next story for the magazine should be exceptionally interesting," Bart Dickerson said. "You're going to love doing it, especially the research."

Karen Samuelson knew Bart was being insincere; he always raised one bushy eyebrow when he was lying. He smiled through his thin lips. Karen's boss at *Person* magazine only smiled when something unpleasant was about to happen to someone. She wasn't one of his favorite people. If writing for the magazine wasn't such a good job for a journalist, she'd have quit long ago. She often had to remind herself there were precious few jobs for journalists these days. She was fortunate to have this one.

"Who am I interviewing?"

"Dr. Jeremy Whitman."

"Never heard of him."

"He's a research anthropologist at Northern State University."

"What's he done that's so significant it warrants an interview?"

"Something dynamic in forensic anthropology."

"How come I never heard of him?"

"That's because he keeps a very low profile. It won't be like any interview you've done before, not like an airhead starlet. There's depth here. I'm giving you the chance of a lifetime."

Karen was still dubious about her boss' words as she drove up to the secluded complex run by Dr. Whitman. She'd left Manhattan on a blustery winter day, flown into Boston and rented a car to drive north. Snow filled the dark wooded forest. Large "No Trespassing" signs were posted everywhere. The high, chain-link, electrified fence that surrounded the ten-acre tract of land looked intimidating.

Karen had to identify herself at the main gate and wait for it to open. The road beyond it was narrow and filled with potholes. Off in the distance, she saw an ugly gray building, and drove toward it. She didn't see any people, and wondered where they might be. Except for the eerie sound whistling through the trees, there was nothing. Strange how accustomed to the city she'd become with its varied cacophony of unique noises.

She knocked at the door, and a man dressed in a plaid flannel shirt and jeans answered. He looked reasonably young, middle to late twenties, clean-cut, wearing rimless eyeglasses.

"I'm here to see Dr. Whitman," she said. "I'm Karen Samuelson, a reporter from *Person* magazine."

"Kevin Marshall, Dr. Whitman's assistant," he said, his handshake damp and limp like a dead fish. "He's expecting you."

There seemed nothing to do but follow him into the building. From the first, she could see it was a Spartan facility. She was offered a cup of coffee that smelled and tasted like something reminiscent of furniture polish remover, but at least it was hot.

"I guess you expect the tour," Kevin Marshall said as they waited for the professor.

"What tour?"

"The body farm . You're being treated like a V.I.P. Dr. Whitman plans to conduct you around personally." Kevin Marshall knifed his hand through a shock of light brown hair. "He really doesn't do it for everyone. In fact, this is the first interview he's ever given for as long as I've known him."

Should she be honored? What had Bart gotten her into this time?

Dr. Whitman turned out to be a large man, fiftyish and nearly bald. His eyes were light blue, cool and distant. He looked at the way she was dressed with clear disapproval. "Those boots are the wrong kind for walking in our woods in the dead of winter."

"I didn't bring any others," she said, wondering why she bothered to sound placating. Something about the man made her uneasy.

"We'll just make allowances then." He smiled at her in a manner that did nothing to alleviate her discomfort.

He led her outside to a walking path. "What questions do you want to ask me?"

"To start with, why do they call this place the body farm?"

"This is the outdoor laboratory of the university's forensic anthropology research facility. At any one time, there are at least fifteen to twenty-five bodies in various stages of decomposition scattered around here."

"Are you serious?" She stared at him with a shocked expression.

"Isn't that why you came here, to do a story on our

unique approach to forensic science?" He studied her thoughtfully. "We are not ghouls. We have a serious purpose here. Law enforcement and forensic medicine students from all over the country come to study the effects of different environments on the decay of bodies. The information we collect is used everywhere, even in foreign countries to investigate all sort sorts of violent deaths and crimes."

"That sounds like a very worthy occupation," she said.

She could imagine Bart's amusement. He knew she hated morbid assignments. Silently, she cursed the man, consigning him to Hell.

Karen followed Dr. Whitman reluctantly down the path. They walked through snow-covered landscape littered with exposed cadavers. There were also body bags with decaying limbs hanging out from several. She felt a visceral tightening and wished she'd skipped breakfast that morning. She didn't want to disgrace herself by throwing up; it was going to be a close call.

"That poor fellow over there was shot to death. There are bullet holes in the skull. He was a victim of violence. Now, the one you see on the other side died peacefully in his sleep. Death is the great equalizer, isn't it? All men are the same here, rich and poor alike."

"You sound like a philosopher."

"I took a few philosophy and psychology courses before turning to forensic medicine."

"Doctor, do you just let these bodies decay out in the open?" She'd never felt so cold in her entire life, zero at the bone.

"That's the idea. We let them rot to skin and bones. I realize the notion of bodies decomposing in this manner may be upsetting, but I assure you that it is critical to understanding death and homicide. Most law enforcement officers have never even seen a dead body." He pointed to another shrunken corpse partly covered by snow. "The dead are shrouded and buried. We don't dwell on what is considered gruesome in our society. It's taboo."

"Where do you get all these bodies?" Karen asked, shaking with chill.

"We have three main sources: first, the unclaimed dead, second, those who have donated their bodies to science, and last, those who specifically state they want their bodies donated to the farm after death. It's all scientifically handled; we tag each corpse so that they can be identified after decomposition."

Karen caught sight of a body partly stuffed into a suitcase. A rusting car held two more corpses, one in the backseat, another with an arm hanging out of a partially open trunk.

"It's good you came on a cold day," the professor said with a grim smile. "When the weather gets warm, the stench is overpowering. The smell of death and decay is quite unforgettable. I'm certain you, as a writer, will think of some fine metaphors and similes for it."

The silence surrounding them was unsettling. The snow-covered woodlands appeared tranquil, yet reminders of death in the form of exposed cadavers were everywhere.

Karen let out a startled gasp. A skeleton stared up at her with a gaping jaw and empty eye sockets, an expression of horror frozen obscenely on his face. Karen stumbled forward hurriedly, slipping on an icy boulder.

"I should caution you to watch your step." The doctor took her arm momentarily.

"It's eerie here." She swallowed hard.

"The early settlers of New England believed the woods were inhabited by demons. I suppose, good Puritans that they were, they feared Native Americans were sent by Satan to test their faith. A certain darkness does permeate these woods. It's almost a preternatural sensation, don't you think? The natural supernatural."

"Why do you have such a high fence around the property? Why the barbed wire and electrification? Surely, you're not afraid of your subjects getting out?"

"No, we're afraid of people coming in, particularly curiosity seekers. Teenagers are a particular problem. We have to be concerned about theft and desecration. There have been incidents. Security is a serious concern at our facility."

They passed another specimen. The doctor lifted a black tarp gently with his gloved hand and exposed the frozen remains of a body. "This one was coming along quite nicely before the temperatures dropped. When it warms again, the maggots will continue doing doing their work, after they've consumed the soft flesh, I usually send out students from the anthropology department to clean up."

"What do you mean by clean up?" she asked uncertainly.

"We send them in wearing protective clothing including plastic gloves and boots. They collect the remains in black, plastic bags and take them to the lab for processing. After the bones have been steamed clean, they are recycled; we respect the life chain. Would you like a tour of the lab as well? It can be arranged? That's Kevin's specialty."

"I-I don't think so. I'm not feeling very well at the moment."

"One becomes desensitized after a time, the way a surgeon who operates must. Have you done any work as a war correspondent or a crime reporter?"

Karen shook her head.

"Pity, you would have been much more accepting of the farm." His voice was gently mocking.

They were joined by Kevin Marshall. Karen felt relieved to see him. "I don't want to bother Dr. Whitman any longer. Maybe you could walk me back to my car? Dr. Whitman, you can just fax your bio to the magazine if you would. I really need to be leaving. I'm afraid I won't be able to write the story about your facility after all. It's just too horrifying."

Dr. Whitman exchanged a considering look with his assistant. "You can still be of use to us, just not in the way in which we originally thought."

He removed an automatic pistol from his coat pocket and pointed it at her chest. Karen stared at him in mute disbelief as sunlight glinted crazily off the barrel.

"What do you think you're doing? Are you crazy?"

"We get so few females here. It would really be helpful to do some comparative studies." His manner seemed almost apologetic.

They intended to kill her for the sake of scientific experimentation? She shook her head uncomprehendingly. "You can't do this. The other people here won't keep quiet."

"At the moment, no one else is about. Spring break for the university. As for the dead, they bear silent witness."

Karen's heart pounded like a hammer against an anvil. "I'm expected back in New York."

"Of course, you are. I'm rather expecting your disappearance will not go unnoticed." The doctor turned to his assistant. "You'll have to leave her rental a good distance from here."

"This is insane. The police will look here for me." She could not control the shrill quality of her voice.

"They won't find you." His voice was maddeningly calm, smooth as maple syrup. "I admit it would be better if this were summer. Mother Nature's little helpers can reduce a fresh body to bones within several weeks when the weather is hot and humid, but we'll manage." He looked sinister, demented.

"What about your story? A magazine article on you and this place, it could make you famous. There'd be more grant money. I believe I was mistaken, I could write the article after all." Surely, a reminder of the original purpose of her visit would turn his mind around.

He smiled at her almost kindly. "I'm afraid not. You see, I've had a change of heart. When your editor called, he was so persuasive, but people won't understand our work here. You just demonstrated that. I have no ego. I don't need fame or fortune. The work I do is what matters and it's what I will leave to posterity, and so, I must bid you farewell, my dear."

"He's crossing the line," she said turning to Kevin Marshall. "You can't let him murder me! Please help me."

The assistant shrugged at her, expressionless.

There was no saliva in her mouth and her throat swelled. She had to escape. She could not stop the trembling in her body. It swayed like the mast of a sailing ship as she stared at the weapon held so steadily in the doctor's hand.

● ● ●

It seemed as if an eternity passed, but it was less than a second. In a flash of white light, she hurled her body into Kevin Marshall, throwing him off-balance and knocking him into Dr. Whitman. Her strength was the effect of an amazing adrenaline rush born of desperation, panic and horror. Karen ran blindly into the woods. She needed to get back to her rental. Thank God, they hadn't taken her handbag! There was a chance for her yet. She could hear them coming after her.

Which direction?

Which way?

Her legs seemed to move of their own volition. Her heart beat like a racehorse approaching the final furlong.

There it was just ahead. She was going to make it. She'd get out of this hellhole, get back to Manhattan and kill her boss for sending her here. Her hands were shaking and her legs were gelatin as she pulled open the car door. Thank God she hadn't bothered to lock it. She almost dropped her handbag and then could scarcely manage to place the key in the ignition. But it worked! The engine roared to life. She locked the doors, and threw the car into drive.

Kevin Marshall hurled himself across her windshield, but she speed up, hit a pothole and sent him flying.

What satisfaction that gave her!

It was short-lived because the gate dead ahead was closed. In her rearview mirror she could see the professor and Kevin still running after her. Kevin was limping but he hadn't given up the pursuit. Dr. Whitman fired and shattered the back window.

Karen knew she had to keep going. Would she be electrocuted when she hit the fence? Cars were grounded by their rubber tires, weren't they? No one in a car ever got hit by lightening, did they? Desperate, she went forward without hesitation.

Blinding white light flashed instantaneous with pain, but it was mercifully over before she could think or react to it. The last thing Karen saw was her mother's face, sweet, smiling with love, just as she'd once been in life. And then—nothing.

● ● ●

"Did you see the way she froze when you shot her the first time? It was like a deer caught in headlights." Kevin Marshall shook his head. "I wonder what she was thinking."

Dr. Whitman bent down, gently touching the young woman's bloody head. The second bullet had ripped through the brain, a perfect death shot. He lifted her limp wrist and felt for a non-existent pulse. "She thought what they all think I suppose—what you and I will think when our time comes. She didn't believe it would actually happen. She couldn't accept it, probably thought she'd escape somehow. All life ends in death, no matter how desperately people wish to cling to it or how they try to delude themselves otherwise." He sighed deeply. "Oh well, time to get on with our work."

Running on Dead Leaves

BY JOHN STEELE

Alex McCutcheon took another step toward the end of the road, fire in his throat and a cold fury raging in his lungs.

The Honeybourne Way was the conclusion of an eight kilometer circuit through a bleary October morning, past the athletic grounds, into Pittville Park for a loop and back. Running was a self-imposed penance on a day this bleak and damp. The earthy smell of dead leaves hung in the fine morning drizzle and a dim haze of mist that smothered the town. He focused on the nip of Bushmills waiting at the end of the punishment.

Honeybourne Way. The name sounded trite, so unlike the harsh, abrasive names of the rabbit-warren of streets where he'd grown up: Centurion Way, Crimea Street, the Shankill Road. It was on those streets he'd smoked the odd Benson and Hedges and swapped whispered tales of the sinister bogeymen of the 'Butchers.' Back in the day, back before the Harrison bar, and Michael Dillon and the Branch, and relocation.

He stepped up his running pace, pushing his burning calves up a steep incline. His eyes focused through on the slick concrete path a couple of yards ahead; he tuned his thoughts to the immediate future three or four steps ahead and exiled the past.

The pain helped occupy his mind. It helped him target the next stretch of the course and jettison thoughts of the previous fifty minutes of strain. It helped banish thoughts further back too, even if it was a losing battle. Memories crept up on him every day, like a ghost runner he fought to stay ahead of, who never tired and always seemed just a couple of steps behind.

He pounded along the concrete, the harsh, rhythmic rasp of his breath reminding him of how cold it was, how hard this was, how alive he was. He made a turn onto the eastern side of Pittville Park.

He thought how different this was to the Hammer Playing Fields where he'd kicked a football— and lumps— out of his mates as a kid. The fields had been a collection of scruffy pitches surrounded by terraced houses bullying in on all sides. The flags hanging from the houses and lamp posts fed his fantasy of playing in front of a packed house at Anfield or Ibrox stadiums. And it was where, as an eighteen year old, he'd become a Black Neck.

* * *

He is standing on the scuffed, scarred pitches, his heart beating faster than it ever has when he runs, staring at the three masked men holding handguns a couple of yards away. The guns are revolvers and he thinks of cowboys and cops and Clint Eastwood. The swearing-in is held in the wee small hours, outside because it's easier to do a runner if the police or army show up. He feels the heft of the Webley & Scott pistol in his hand as he takes his vows—smells the gun oil and the booze on the commander's breath. After, they all get hammered in a shebeen in a small clubhouse with the windows bricked up and a camera on the door, Belfast style. He is blind drunk on Bushmills and poteen and watches a couple of the other lads get tattoos on their arms to celebrate. As the sun comes up on a crisp August morning, he lies on the grass in the Hammer fields and looks up at the sinuous clouds, a fully paid up member of the Ulster Volunteer Force.

• • •

Pittville Park couldn't have been more different from west Belfast. It was a genteel, sculpted throwback to another, more refined age. As he completed a circuit of the ornamental lake and crossed an elegant stone bridge, he glanced at the huge Regency townhouses lining the eastern side of the lawns. In the autumnal gloom, one small light burned fiercely through the semi-darkness on top of a looming four-story monstrosity, all pillars and austere Roman façade. It looked small and vulnerable atop the dark forest of black windows below and he imagined such a cavernous old house might contain its share of secrets.

All was quiet and he could hear the coarse rasp of his breath, harsh and rhythmic, as he continued at a steady pace, a cloud of condensation billowing around him as his feet impacted on the path. He ran toward the narrow foot tunnel burrowing under the Evesham Road, little more than a black cave in the half-light. He almost halted on the approach on the eastern side, the jolt of his trainers on the path pummeling his knees. A black, shambling shadow dragged its bulk through the murk in the tunnel ahead. Alex heard a pig-like scuffing and snorting.

• • •

The man had been hard once, in line to be a Chief of

Staff. Now, the hardest thing about him is the wrist bone spearing through the skin of the broken joint. His breath rasps and snuffles through his broken nose and split lips. He takes shambling steps as he hauls his broken bulk with weary resignation.

He is a grass, a tout, a police informer.

The boys in the lower Shankill beat him, getting the names of his handlers and those he'd informed on. Now he is spent, both as a source of information and as a human being. The man moves on, choosing the direction of the cliff edge as his ultimate goal, probably aware this is the end. There is not another soul as far as the eye can see on the windswept Antrim plateau. Alex watches Sharkey stride up to the back of the man's skull and pump four rounds into it. The muzzle flashes form a downward arc as Sharkey's hand follows the falling body to the ground.

Alex shudders and tells himself it is the cold. He is glad he didn't pull the trigger.

• • •

The shape was an old lady; the sound, her West Highland Terrier. A local resident out walking her dog on a dreary English morning.

Alex passed her and emerged from the other end of the tunnel onto the path around the boating pond on the western side. The park widened out here. The houses were a good distance off across the expanse of grass to his left, the pond and modest golf links to his right. He'd never seen fish in the pond, but supposed there must be some. Shadows flitted below the darkened surface, between the dead and fallen leaves floating there. Alex passed the grasping tangle of unkempt bushes and wildflowers where he'd seen a couple of kids poking a dead cat with a stick last month. The stalking husk of a climbing frame loomed ahead as he neared the deserted children's playground, the weedy shafts and angles emerging from the early morning gloom.

And then he stopped.

He saw a house on the verge of an expanse of grass to his left that he'd never noticed before. In all the months that he'd been running this course, he'd never realized it was there. Alex shook his head in consternation.

The house stood alone, a short way inside the park's far boundary, a slash of red brick against the cream-colored backs of the row of Regency townhouses that edged the western reaches of this stretch of the park, apparent even through the October gloom. It faced in toward the green space, away from its neighbors. A Victorian red brick structure. It had no fence or wall, but a couple of threadbare trees that might screen it from the park when green and verdant in summer. A blanket of rotting leaves lay scattered at the approach to the entrance. Years of re-pelling the British weather had given it a rusted, spoiled look, but enough of the original, ruddy texture of the brick shone through to give it a sense of warmth in the chilly mist of rain now starting. Alex peered through the damp air and saw the gable wall nearest him was windowless and there was a dirty grey discoloration smeared across it.

He realized he was jogging across the damp grass toward the house and his running shoes, all a hundred and forty quid of them, were soaked. The shoes were state-of-the-art: Japanese made with hundreds of tiny little perforations to allow his feet to breathe as he battered them on the ground. Today the pores were saturating them instead. He was now a couple of meters from the house.

He saw that the discoloration was actually a mural that had faded through the years, so it looked like the ghost of a tattoo. Hard to know what someone would want to paint on a gable wall in Cheltenham, but no doubt it was a better class of mural than the terrorist representations on the Shankill.

• • •

There is a Saltire and an Ulster flag, flanking a furious-looking figure whose hands are wrapped around the stock and barrel of an AK-47. The angry portrait and its background covers the entirety of the brick wall. Sharkey stands at the foot of this raging giant smoking a cigarette and glancing at his watch. When he sees Alex, a broad smile splits his face.

• • •

Abruptly, he shook his head. Why was he doing this? Why was he approaching the house?

Why hadn't he just noted the structure and run on?

They'd always told him to be alert to anomalies in the everyday, especially the big peeler, Orr. But that would be more like a stranger walking a dog or a parked car that looked out of place.

Not a bloody building.

Alex thought himself foolish. He only came to the park when he was running and had probably been so focused on his pace and time that he'd never really taken in his surroundings.

But as he studied the house he saw he was not looking at a faded mural, but a cluster of small, circular marks.

- ka-thump! –

They were round bruises, about two metres in height.

- ka-thump! ka-thump! -

He walked closer, conscious of the fact that the owner might not take kindly to a sweating, heaving stranger scouting the outside of their home.

- ka-thump! ka-thump! -

Now he could see a pattern on the marks, mucky hexagons peppering each circle: footballs.

• • •

He hears the rhythmic, almost measured thump and bounce of kids knocking a ball against the gable wall on Riga Street: ka-thump! ka-thump! The gable wall of The Harrison bar. He can hear the sounds because a window is ajar in the upstairs room where he and the others are smoking, drinking tea and talking football on a bright summer evening. The upstairs room where a broken, ragged figure sits slumped and unconscious in a wooden chair, smeared in blood with a pool of piss at its feet. The stench of ammonia is rank. The room where, after getting the directive from Brigade Staff, they will finally finish Dillon.

They'd picked him up in Sharkey's car, made him think he was taking a taxi. They told themselves he was a Provo, but deep down they knew he was just some fella from the Falls. But somebody has to pay for the five dead in the bombing and if they can't get the bomber, this boy will do. Poor fucker cried his eyes out in the motor, pissed himself before Parky started on him with a chunk of wood he picked up from the mouth of the old fireplace on the wall to their left. The screaming and pleading pierced the murmur and muted laughter and clink of glasses coming from the bar downstairs.It went on for an age. Once Dillon is beaten so badly he can't speak, his teeth scattered across the carpet like broken Lego bricks, they open the window to ease the smell of sweat, blood and urine that corrupts the air. Alex hasn't touched the fella yet. Then the word comes from on high, downstairs, to finish the job and Sharkey hands him the gun and Alex puts a couple of bullets in Dillon's head.

• • •

Back to the here and now. Concentrate on the now. Concentrate on the house.

It had one bay window to the left of the front door and a couple of smaller windows on the first floor. He could sense no signs of life in the place and quietly edged around to the front for a better look. The curtains in the bay windows were drawn and tied back, although the room was in deep shadow in the dim autumnal light. From this angle he could make out little other than a few greasy marks smeared down the window. They were more prominent as he walked closer, like smudged scars on the dusty glass, and they looked strangely obscene against the dense inner murk of the room beyond.

• • •

There weren't any windows in the cell when the RUC had picked them all up for the shooting. For hours, the cops beat, goaded, and threatened him. Now, Special Branch are here and it's all cups of tea and updates on the football results.

They never use the term informant.

The big one, Gordon Orr, said, "It's all about saving lives, Alex. Give us the Shankill Brigade staff and we'll give you a new life across the water. Safe as houses."

It is a second chance. If he can't stop the dreams – the

nightmares – about Dillon, at least he can put some distance between himself and the past. He tells them about Mandrake and Simpson and the other paramilitaries. They'll be locked up and he'll be where?

• • •

So here he is. Those he'd imprisoned had their freedom anyway – amnesty thanks to the peace process – and he had a new life: daily runs, organic food, and walks with the dog on Leckhampton Hill.

And now this house.

With a couple more steps, he was at the door. Twin eyes of frosted glass daring him to look inside. He peered through the dimpled texture of the glazing. Something scuttled past from within. It was so brief, so fleeting, that all he caught was a phantom shadow in his mind's eye, like a blur on a photograph taken on the run. He shivered in the early morning chill and told himself he was cooling down due to the break in his run.

Alex was no fool. He'd spent enough time in a hard place to know when to wade in and when to cut his losses and walk away. He was also a believer in fate. Fate was arbitrary and impartial; it didn't care for religion or sex or race or guilt or innocence. He supposed he had relocated to Cheltenham because it was fate. He had dragged his carcass out of bed to run, and his run had brought him to this spot, and he was standing in front of this house, thanks to fate.

He was cold, exhausted, and unnerved by what he'd just seen, but he was also tired of being scared. He was tired of the daily fear of exposure, of discovery, and of looking over his shoulder that touting had brought. And anyway, this was well-bred Cotswolds-England on a grey and non-descript October morning. Morning, for God's sake.

So he tried the door handle and, much to his unease, it gave and swung inward.

He scolded himself as another, involuntary shiver spasmed down his spine. Alex glanced back for reassurance and saw the dark abyss of the lake and the skeletal wraiths of the trees through the gloom. Then he calmed his heart and stepped inside.

The entrance hall was gloomy and soundless, and the air thick with stale decay, as if the place had been derelict for an age. A faded Persian hall carpet lay over a diamond patterned, tiled floor and the end of the hall was cloaked in shadow: a dark place. He glanced up at the staircase to his right, the top devoid of light or life. Maybe later, he thought.

He resolved to check the front room. His footsteps made no sound as he made his way to the open door on the left. Despite the apparent age of the place there were no creaking floorboards, the gripes and moans of the old house settling. It was totally still.

He stepped into the front room, dimly lit by the tarnished autumn sky outside. It was sparsely furnished with an empty cast-iron Victorian fireplace against the far wall and an austere oak table opposite it on the right of the doorway. There were three empty wooden chairs, arranged in a semi-circle around the silent howl of the dead hearth.

Alex took another couple of steps and squinted at the bay window. The scene was as expected: the grass, the dull canopy of the sky, the balding trees standing in a ragged matting of dead leaves out front. But there was something about the glass. He whispered to himself, scolding himself for failing to concentrate and then it came to him. The glass was clear of smears or smudges. The marks he had seen outside had vanished.

The front door slammed and his heart lurched.

Pain seared his chest but he barely noticed as a wild panic swallowed him. It was like running, the mind shutting down as motor function took over and he covered the short distance to the hall and the door; not thinking, just acting. He pulled on the handle, wrenching it. Adrenaline coursed through his system, panic rising. The door was stuck fast. He kicked it, hammered it, cursed it. But the door was adamant.

He heard noise upstairs. Deliberate footsteps making their way across the ceiling, the landing, toward that terrible black space at the top of the staircase.

- *"Go on, Alex."* -

- *"Time to earn your spurs."* -

And more, the soft murmur of voices in another room, a clinking of glasses. A braying laugh and someone shouting for attention.

- *"Shoot the bastard."* -

- *"Nobody'll hear. The noise of the bar downstairs'll swallow the gunshot."* -

A fresh wave of panic surged through him, driving him back to the front room and the bay window. He grabbed a chair and hurled it at the glass. It rebounded wildly, forcing him to spasm madly to avoid it, and splintered on the metallic edge of the fireplace. The snapping sound it made was accompanied by something else.

- *ka-thump!* -

A rhythmic slap, like leather on brick.

- *ka-thump!* -

A football.

- *ka-thump! thump!* -

The slap of the football mingled with another dull rhythmic beat. Then the sound of the football was gone and all that remained was a tread on the stairs. It grew louder, crowding and stifling the air, despite the roar of surging blood in Alex's ears, and he wondered madly why his own frantic steps were still so silent.

Somewhere he heard a cry – *"No, Jesus, please! No!"* -

There was a violent, sharp, wet sound and an ugly laugh. He stared at the open door to the front room and saw a dark mass of shadow advance down the wall next to the stairs, and across the carpet in the hall. It was disembodied and Alex felt his own body go cold as he waited for someone, something, to follow that dark shape which now swallowed the hallway and advanced on the verge of the room he stood rooted in.

- *"No! I have a wife! No!"* -

He could smell cigarette smoke and spilt beer. The sharp stench of piss pierced the air. And something squalid and metallic: Blood.

- *"I have a kid, please! A wee girl!"* -

The stench brought the strength of madness to his limbs and he hurled another chair. A leg smashed on the window pane itself.

- *"Oh, Christ, you're going to kill me!"* -

The footsteps were in the hall.

- *"I'm dead, aren't I?"*

The room darkened around him as he scrabbled at the window. His greasy fingers smearing violent stains down the glass with screams of protest. Through the dying light, he saw the woman with the dog on the path a way off.

The dog was sniffing at a disheveled heap. He realized the woman was screaming silently as she stood over the lifeless body of a runner in expensive-looking shoes, lying on the concrete at her feet.

Dreaming of Honey

BY J.M. PERKINS

Megan flipped through glossy gossip magazine as the TV buzzed inanities behind her. She really should have unsubscribed from the auto-renewal, but she somehow convinced herself that money wasn't *that* tight. Never mind that she was underwater on the mortgage. Never mind that she didn't have an entertainment budget to speak of. Never mind that she didn't know how she was going to pay the credit card minimums next month. By god, she could still afford a fucking magazine, even if it meant getting one of those overdraft fees.

If only she hadn't let the agent talk her into buying the condo. But after everything, she'd be damned if she was going to lose it. Keeping the condo and her dog were just about all she cared about anymore.

Cobo—her great, dumb, ten-year-old mound of a Golden Labrador—rolled his shoulders. A shivering wave of fur passed over his body. The dog opened his mouth and green liquid roiled onto the much abused condo carpet. Megan stared at the scene, startled, concerned about her dog, but more curious than anything. When he finished, she knelt to pet him. "You ok, Boy?"she asked, concern in her voice. Megan had to jerk back to keep Cobo from licking her face.

"Down!"

Something twitched in the pool of vomit.

Megan couldn't quite make out the moving bits. They seemed to be a darker clump amongst the bile. She leaned closer. The dog took the opportunity to wag his tail and hop up on the couch.

"NO, Cobo. Down," she said, pushing the enthusiastic lab away. She looked back at the brown figures in the green. Tiny half-digested legs spasmed in the puddle. Three bees in various stages of digestion writhed about in the vomit.

"Ewww."

Cobo kept wagging his tail, happy that he didn't feel sick anymore.

• • •

On Monday, she found four dead bees on the floor. Had this sort of thing been happening for a while? Had Cobo had been 'disposing' of the evidence? She got out the broom and dustbin to sweep up the insects, dumped them in the trash. She ended up forgetting all about it as she watched reality TV, absently scratching at Cobo's furry head.

• • •

Tuesday, she decided to do something about the problem. Five more bees had gotten into her apartment. Three of them were dead, but the surviving pair buzzed about the living room, moshing against her window. She waved a broom around the air in an awkward imitation of a killing strike, managing to down one of the little bastards before it had a chance to sting.

She missed the second bee, angering it. The insect

landed, pressed its stinger to Megan's lower thigh. The hot pin-prick of pain made her bite her lip. The bee wafted off to die, half its guts clinging to the poison sack stuck into Megan. She bared her teeth as she plucked the painful spear from her goose-pimpled skin before icing the spot. She cleaned up all the other carapaces and put 'call home-owner's association - bees' on her to-do list.

She spent the next half hour rubbing away the pain in her leg. Her shows didn't distract her quite as well that night, and Cobo was acting like he was sick.

● ● ●

The next day Megan called Carl, president of the Home Owner's Association, from her cluttered cubicle at the office. Every minute or so, she would look around to see if Mr. Ottley had spotted her making personal calls on company time.

"Hey, this is Megan…" she said when the call connected.

"Oh, hey," Carl said. Megan realized he had no idea who she was. She didn't know how many times she'd introduced herself.

"Megan Bethany… over at unit 5?"

"Oh, of course."

"Yeah, uh huh, I got a problem."

"Oh?"

"Well, I think there's a hive of bees on my property. Or outside really, but they keep getting into the house. Can you hire someone? To take care of this?"

"Hmmm, well. Are you sure they're exterior? Because if not then they're not really a Home Owner's Association issue."

"Wait, what? Of course they're outside, they're bees! Don't try to weasel out of this. This is why I pay my HOA dues!"

"Well, ok. How about this: how about you hire an exterminator and when they take care of the issue and confirm this is an exterior maintenance issue, we'll reimburse you."

Megan sucked in breath, "Ok, I'm going to be completely honest here. I don't really have the money to do this, even if you reimburse me."

Silence reigned, and for a moment Megan was worried he had hung up on her.

"Ok, well I'll try to convince the board to outlay the money. We meet next week."

"But this is an emergency! What if I was allergic?"

"Are you allergic?"

"Well, no but…"

Megan took in a long breath through her mouth, snorted it out her nose like they'd taught her in yoga. 'You're fine.' She thought to herself.

"Well, fine! Do what you can… but please hurry! I'm not allergic or anything but I don't want to come home every night to an apartment full of bees."

• • •

Thursday, Megan unlocked the front door. She hoped that the problem somehow might have fixed itself. Frustrated bees buzzed inside the small apartment, maybe fifteen in all. They seemed to be fixated around the windows, which was good because it meant they weren't swarming her.

Cobo ran up whimpering, jumping to her thigh. She

said "Come here." She knelt down and pet him. "It's ok, boy." She led him to the bathroom while she said soothing things. She didn't take her eyes off the buzzing things.

Another dozen bees seemed to have died about the apartment, most boiled alive in troughs around light bulbs. The living, stinging insects spun about the air, looking for the source of their distress. Megan took the recently purchased a can of wasp spray out of her bag and proceeded to murder anything that moved.

She stalked around the condo, dousing the bastards. The haze of chemical tang made her nose twist up. Megan reminded herself it was worse for the bees. After a few more sprays, she began to appreciate the sound.

Bugs dead, she called Carl back and screamed at his answering machine. She thought about calling her mother and asking for money enough to stay in a hotel or to hire the exterminator herself. But no, she still hadn't paid her back from last time. And it would be just like her mother to start picking at her about her move to the city, about her 'acting,' about everything.

She didn't need that tonight.

Megan decided to keep herself occupied, and walked into the kitchen. As the fresh chopped onions and potatoes sizzled in the large skillet, Megan could hear faint buzzing from above her head. She put her ear to the vent hood.

"My god..." Megan said to no one. "They built a hive in the vent."

She ran for her half roll of duct tape, and spent fifteen minutes sealing all the open spaces above the range where a bee could conceivably squeeze through. She called Carl's answering machine again, left an updated rant. As Megan worked, Cobo whined and scratched at the bathroom door.

• • •

Megan did her best to sleep in the car, but eventually gave up; she couldn't get comfortable. Resigned to sleeping in her bed, she double-checked the vent hood and fortified her room. She closed the sliding glass to the patio, shoving towels around the cracks.

"Up, Cobo. Up." She said, inviting Cobo onto the bed.

She snuggled up to him appreciating the comfort of his earthy dog stink. Pride or no pride, nagging or no nagging, she would call Mom tomorrow and beg for some money. She wouldn't spend another night here.

When sleep finally overtook her, her dreams were full of honey pots with dollar signs on them.

• • •

Fire. That's what her leg felt like. She bolted upright in the bed, clawing at the burning pain. She clicked on the bedside lamp, pulled up her pajama bottoms and turned her thigh to see an inch wide red welt. From its center, clear liquid oozed. "Damnit." She poked at the wound. It split open like a mouth.

In the hole in her leg, a furry infant bee face stared back out at her. Megan screamed and began to dig with her nails at the wound and the nestled bug within. The bee retreated deeper to avoid her.

She screamed and cursed and tore, breaking three of her short, acrylic nails before she finally excavated the bug and the surrounding tissue. But there was more; it looked yellow in there. She shoved her fingernails back into her trembling flesh, terror making her almost numb to the pain.

Pinching her fingers together, blood spurting out all over the sheets, Megan drew a waxy cylinder out of the wound in her leg. It smelled of honey and blood.

She drove to the hospital in a blur.

Only later, sitting on bed in an assless hospital gown, filling out her insurance information, did she remember that Cobo was still in the apartment.

• • •

Questions came after an abrupt examination and some stitches to pull together the crude wound. She confirmed that the gash was self inflicted, but all the doctors wanted to know why she had done it to herself. No matter how many times she told them, they didn't believe her.

They asked, 'Why did you hurt yourself?' And she told them, over and over again. Hell, they could come back to the apartment and look. All the while Cobo was trapped in the condo with the *bees*.

Finally, she lied and they let her go. It was the end of the night shift and they had other issues to deal with. But by then the sun had risen and Cobo had been alone in the apartment all night.

• • •

All she wanted was to crawl away to some hotel and hire someone to firebomb the condo. But she couldn't; she had to save Cobo and then the Condo, in that order. As she drove, she called everyone she could think of who might help her. Lots of voicemails. Some sleep-addled acquaintances promised to help... as soon as they woke up, as soon as they got dressed; but not now. They could get there later in the afternoon, after work.

Megan would have to do this alone. She approached her condo, wearing the same nearly indecent bloodstained pajamas she had rushed to the hospital in. She sat in the car breathing hard for four minutes before she summoned the courage to get out.

Megan walked up to her front door. She placed a hand on the knob, afraid to turn it as though she were checking for heat from a fire. The air beyond the wood thrummed with a thousand tiny voices. She ran back to her car, pulled on the scrubby salt-stained sweats she had worn last week at the gym.

Pulling the strings of her hoodie tight, Megan opened the door.

"Cobo," she called, praying that he would run to her, praying that she wouldn't have to enter the apartment. No response except the incessant insect noise. Dark shapes darted about in the dim morning light. She sucked in air. She would do this slow, take her time. They wouldn't attack her unless she spooked them. Right?

She walked past the kitchen, The bees had chewed through the duct tape around the range hood. Honey and wax slimed down through the black metal above the burners.

Megan crossed the threshold to the bedroom, the screen of bees growing thicker. She could barely think, the buzzing was so loud. She found what was left of Cobo whimpering in the corner.

The hive had been busy with the dog. Dozens of the insects darted in and out of a symmetrical series of wounds in his back leg. They'd built honeycomb around the dog's tendons, burrowed holes along his thigh. Everything dripped yellow and red as tiny, still wet bees flew for the first time. Megan struggled to keep herself from retching. 'Breathe.' She told herself as she walked over to Cobo. Her fingers trembled as she reached down for her dog.

"It's ok, Cobo. It's gonna be ok."

Megan lifted her dog and held him close, something she hadn't been really able to do since he was a puppy and a good sixty pounds lighter. Movement disturbed the new hive. The haze of pheromones shifted. Agitated bees began to land on Megan. They clung to her, trying to sting through her clothing to reach the soft skin underneath. Some targeted her hands and feet, puckering her flesh with their venom and eggs.

Clutching Cobo, Megan ran; grunting with effort of carrying a fifty pound dog. The lab whined and tried to lick her face. Every few seconds, she felt another prick on her on a finger or along her heel. Her feet and hands began to swell, grow numb. Cobo yelped, bees landing all over his body.

Before she got through the door, three bees had managed to get through to her face, stinging her ear, her forehead, and above her left eye. Megan managed to stagger the half staircase to the car. Fumbling to beep open the Honda, she tossed Cobo onto the passenger seat and slammed the door. She couldn't keep her hands from shaking, and her left eye was swollen till it was nothing more than a slit. She couldn't get the key into the ignition. Megan lost consciousness before she could release the parking brake.

For hours after, hundreds of bees battered themselves against the car windows.

• • •

Neighbors called, huddling behind closed windows. A team of emergency exterminators arrived, trucks unloaded men in bee suits who wandered about the parking lot like low-rent astronauts in a low budget 50's sci-fi movie. They filled the air with poison, killing bees by the hundreds.

Paramedics brought Megan to the hospital, leaving the corpse of the dog to be thrown away by a neighbor when its stink seeped out of the car. She slept as sterile machines blinked and beeped around her. The eggs needled into her hands and feet, incubating, waiting to erupt. Within a week, two hives would hatch: one in the center of Everlasting Mercy Hospital, and one in the city dump around Cobo's body.

Megan twitched and murmured. Bees battered themselves against the hospital's window as she dreamt of honey.

Cats for Ginger

BY Mathew Allan Garcia

It was after midnight when I realized no one would come and do it for me, that I was all alone and my little sister was likely dead, or worse.

The shotgun on my lap weighed down on me, as though it were getting heavier every second I put it off. I wore the knee-high boots Mom left behind, a facemask atop my head. I zipped up my leather jacket to my neck, hiding the bruises, the long scars between my breasts, and arms. The Velcro of my workout gloves was pulled tight, fingers pale from gripping the metal barrel shaft.

I was ready.

The creak of the floorboards from Gran's bedroom upstairs started up again, on that rocking chair of hers. Of course the thing sitting in it wasn't Gran, not anymore. I could feel her stare down at me through the wall, down the stairs, and into my room, fire roiling around behind her eyes, smoldering like coals at the bottom of a pit, licking at what little was left to burn.

I reckon before the night's done, I won't be the same anymore either. Though who and what I'll be is to be seen.

That part's not yet written.

●●●

Mom left my little sister, Jess, and I the morning after Thanksgiving. Ginger, the cat, too.

I walked into the kitchen to tell Gran that I didn't think she was comin' back, but by the time I walked up to her, I didn't see the sense in it anymore. Mom had gone up and left several times before. The most recent time on the back of a motorcycle with a man who reeked of car exhaust and called me sugar in a way I didn't much like. I remember the rumbling of the revving motor, and the guilt in my mom's voice, go back inside with Gran, hon. I'll be right back.

Gran was finishing up washing the dishes, Ginger making eights at her feet, rubbing up against her legs. One look at my eyes and Gran knew. Sighing, she looked out the window for a second—her brow bearing the weight of an expression that said she was done being surprised by her daughter's choices.

Gran's hair had begun to gray a few years back, but now it was a deep shade of too-shiny violet, the kind all the women her age seemed to favor. Her white apron billowed out with the breeze smelling of lilac.

Ginger, starved for attention, hopped up onto the counter so Gran would pick her up.

Turning to me she said, "How do you feel about chocolate chip pancakes today, honey? I think it might do us both some good."

It took mom two years to come back that time. In those two years Jess got old enough to know that mom didn't want to fuss around with us. Sometimes Jess would creep into my bed at night, curl up beside me. When I woke up, her pillow was damp with tears and her eyes were two fist-sized balls of pain.

• • •

My mother's boots thudded on the wooden stairs, my heart beating up my throat. My Grandfather's gun was heavy at my side, his giant slayer. When drunk enough, he turned boastful, claiming it could down a damned bear, if given the chance.

The thought comforted me as I reached the top of the stairs. Although the thing that had taken residence in his home, in Gran herself, was something different. I wondered if he'd stand resolutely behind his claim in the face of it.

• • •

When Ginger began to age, Gran decided to get her more cats.

"She's just lonely, is all," she said, rubbing her hands together worriedly.

Ginger gazed indifferently at Jess and I, taking swipes at us if we got too close to Gran. We both agreed the cat wasn't right.

One morning, as I was drawing myself a bath, sleep still in my eyes, I was jolted by Jess's blood curdling scream.

Ginger had brought her a present.

A dead bird, left on her pillow. Its neck hung in an unnatural angle, its body twitching, wings flapping against the sheets. Three pin sized droplets of blood on Jess's pillowcase.

Often we'd wake up in the early morning hours to find Ginger sitting on our room's windowsill, her eyes two shiny coins in the moonlight and a guttural, rumbling growl in her throat. Just staring.

She was fine with Gran though. Sometimes, I thought Gran saw a bit of mom in her eyes. An extension of her, anyway. And while Gran was never mean to Jess and I, she had a way about her. A disconnected way, like she expected us to run off any second, like mom did. Like our grandfather did.

In Gran's eyes, Ginger was the only constant.

• • •

Walking down the hall was like being swallowed by a dying animal. There was only darkness, the odor of fermenting cat shit, and the sound of my boots crunching on month-old cat litter. Feces lined the hall.

There were no windows to show me there was a world outside.

An urge to go back downstairs, grab Gran's keys and drive, gripped me. For a second I closed my eyes, breathed in that putrid air, and steadied my thundering heart. Jess is in there, I thought. I gotta try

At Gran's bedroom door, the stench was palpable. I rolled down my face mask and turned the knob.

• • •

After Ginger passed on, Gran had a collection of thirteen cats—all for Ginger. All wild-eyes and claws because Gran never showed them affection. They were Ginger's companions after all. When the orange tabby went missing for that final time, Gran looked for her everywhere. Walked up the road calling her name. Cried for days. Jess and I helped by lookin' out back, atop the shed roof and along the railroad tracks. Among the campfires of the homeless, where feral cats sometimes hunted for leftover scraps of food.

It was Jess that found Ginger in the crawlspace under the house. She laid curled up in a corner, too far for us to reach, but close enough to see that she was on her way out. The cat cried out, her head bobbing as she turned to us weakly. Her joints and muscles beginning to stiffen, beginning their death rituals, their funeral songs.

Gran got on all fours and crawled in without a second thought. We never volunteered to go and she never asked. Scraping underneath, her mass blocked out all light as she pushed under beams. All we saw was blackness. We heard her pushing aside gravel and the sound of her labored breathing.

When she came to where Ginger was lying, there was little light. We could see the outline of Gran's face through a grate. She wrapped her arms around Ginger's body, nuzzled her face into the cat's fur, whispering her name over and over.

When the faint sound of Gran's sobs reached us, we decided it was time to go in.

● ● ●

Days went by and Gran wasn't the same anymore. Jess said it was Ginger's loss, but the fire was already kindling somewhere in our grandmother's eyes. She went through the motions, hardly talking to us. Then the day came when she went up to her room, and didn't come out.

I searched the cabinets to make Jess and I something to eat. It got to the point where we was low and neither of us wanted to go into Gran's room. Sometimes we'd wake up to find Gran standing in our room, looking out through the window. Her eyes were silver coins, a low rumbling in her throat, where something had taken hold, had eaten up what was Gran. Then one morning, Jess was gone too.

• • •

The Greeks used to put coins on their dead before they were buried to keep their bodies from stirring, the coins were meant to pay the fare for the ferry across the river Styx into Hades. In Scandinavia, the shoes of the dead were bound together, to stop their souls from wandering back into the world of the living. In the end, the final moments in someone's life are its own, and to interfere—to meddle in those final moments—was to look for trouble.

A cat's final moments are its own too, I suppose—a time for it leave its physical shell, to join the cycle once more—and commit itself to the ground. I think Gran took it as a pet sparing her master the sight of it suffering, when she violated that moment, she disrupted Ginger's crossing into the unknown. Something happened down there that night, because there were penalties.

There was no better proof of that than the eyes that stared at me from the rocking chair in Gran's bedroom. Her eyes were hot coals in a sea of black, her hair smoke—wiry and gray. Gran smiled, bloody gums with tiny jagged incisors and large canines, sharp and yellow. Her eyes drew down to slits, fingernails long as pocket-knives, curved at the tips. They clicked on the chair's worn wooden arm.

She closed her eyes, inhaled deeply and smiled.

In the corners of the room, I noticed small coin slot-shaped eyes. Jess groaned on the bed, turning on her side, a congregation of squinting eyes all around her.

One of them lunged at me from the side. I pulled up the shotgun's butt hard, cracking the cat's skull and sending it to the floor with a thump. Another flew at me, knocking me against the wall. Its claws sank into my jacket, gripping and ripping, moving up toward my face.

Gran chuckled, a wet sound, her gums smacking together.

Claws poked through the jacket, through my armor, and I cried out. "Jess—"

Out of the shadows, Gran lunged at me, quick and agile. Her claws splayed out, aiming for my eyes. I dodged out of the way, pulling the cat off of me with my free hand and tossed it at her.

It landed on Gran's face. She stumbled back, her chuckles turning to agony. Crashing into the window, glass peppered the floor. The coin slot eyes move in on me. Gran peeled the cat off, dark rivulets of blood staining her face, smearing across her mouth like lipstick.

The corners of her mouth pulled into a smile, her teeth stained red. She spit a piece of flesh at my feet as she stepped towards me, nails clicking together like hollow bones.

I brought the barrel up.

The expression on her face made me pause. Her eyebrows raised in a familiar expression of my grandmother's disapproval and surprise.

The monster sighed, mock sadness, and the voice that came out of its lips was nearly Gran:

"How does chocolate chip pancakes sound to you, hon? That sound good? Got all the pancakes you'd want." She clicked her teeth together, blood spattering. Her breath reeked of rancid meat and ammonia. "I think Jess—"

I pulled the trigger. It was the sound of my sister's name that made me do it.

Gran fell through the window frame, flying backwards in a mass of splintered wood and glass. Her cats scrambled after her.

• • •

I whispered in Jess's ear, I love you. I love you. I love you.

She groaned, mumbling something I couldn't quite hear, the ringing in my ears drowning out her words.

But I was afraid of what I'll see when she opens her eyes.

Roiling fire.

Smoldering coals.

• • •

I followed Gran's trail alongside the road into town to a dried up part of Murphy's Creek. In the summer, when the snow melt from the mountains filled it up, Jess and I spent our days there. It was morning and the wind was brisk, my jacket still sticking to my flesh.

A mile away from the house I found where she'd ended up. There was blood, lots of it. Alongside her footprints, a dozen or so smaller ones—an exodus of cats.

Eventually the trail ran dry at the mouth of a cave on the riverbank. The cave was three feet wide and almost as tall, just big enough for someone to crawl into. I almost passed it by, its opening hidden by fountain grass. A stagnant, algae—ridden pond sat at its base.

For a moment, I considered following. I pulled out two silver coins from my pants pocket, my hands shaking, and set them on the mouth of the cave.

Serving Justine

BY EDDIE MCNAMARA

Ingredients:

1 bone-in pretty girl thigh, skin on (about 7 pounds)
1 head of garlic cloves, roasted
½ cup fresh oregano
7 tablespoons Kosher salt
1 tablespoon coarsely ground black pepper
3 tablespoons canola oil
2 tablespoons white wine vinegar
750 ML bottle Evan Williams Whiskey
Plastic Wrap
Butcher's Twine
5 whole cloves (optional)

Advance Prep:

1. The infliction of emotional pain is a crucial element in the raising of human livestock for slaughter. Sadness is the sixth and most delicate of tastes—almost imperceptible to your receptors. Unlike sweetness, sourness, bitterness, saltiness or umami, a thoroughly refined palate is required to savor sadness.

2. Do not confuse sadness with fear. Fear tastes bitter, but not bitter in a good way like dandelion greens or radic-

chio. It's bitter like beer that's gone bad from being left out in the sun for too long.

3. If your moral compass guides you away from farm raised meat, or you fancy yourself a hunter, it is of the utmost importance that you choose wild game that you are most physically attracted to. Placing a forbidden part of a sexy person in your mouth is arousing; the same act with an ugly or plain-looking person can lead to stomach upset.

4. Race does not affect taste. However, fat content is vitally important. What you're looking for is skinny-fat. Aim for the perfect 1970s bikini body, rather than the more muscular contemporary female ideal of the post-Beyoncé world. Muscularity leads to toughness and an unpleasant mouth feel, while plus sized gals are often too greasy and soft to serve after cooking. It's a sin to waste food.

Instructions:

1. Using a chef's knife, score the meat by making 3" long diagonal slits in the thigh

2. Combine the roasted garlic, salt, oil, oregano and vinegar in a bowl. Whisk together to create an adobo paste.

3. Massage the roasted garlic adobo into the soft flesh. Be sure to penetrate the slits in the skin with the mixture. Meditate on the word "slit". Play the record "Typical Girl" by The Slits to remind you of her. They were her favorite band. Stop the record. Her favorite band was X-Ray Spex; she wore a vest with a Slits patch when you picked her up. Play the "Oh Bondage! Up Yours!" record. Take care to evenly coat the entire thigh in a

paste of roasted garlic. Admire your work while thinking a pure thought about the source of your protein.

4. Once in the oven, the adobo will form a crust on the outside of the thigh. Remember back when the thigh belonged to a crusty punk. Crusty girls, hitch hikers, runaways and traveller chicks taste the best. They're predisposed to saltiness and bitterness (the good kind) from their world-weariness, and who else is willing to hop into a stranger's car? Remember her name: Justine Libertine. Remember her boa constrictor lips, her fortuneteller blonde dye-job with heavy black roots, and her naïve willingness to accept a ride because you were playing a Patsy Cline tape on your car stereo, and how she said, "Dangerous folks don't listen to 'I Fall to Pieces.'"

5. Fall to pieces.

6. Cover the thigh with plastic wrap and bind it with the butcher's twine. Place in the refrigerator and allow to marinate for at least 3 hours.

7. Do not allow the plastic wrap to trigger any memories of the plastic covered slaughter room. You must not blame yourself. She forced you to do it.

8. Open the whiskey bottle, take liberal pulls from it and marinate yourself in the booze, allowing it to dull your pain. You could have loved her. No, you did love her, but she loved freedom more than she loved you back. Think of all the times you awoke from fright in the middle of the night, checking to see if she was still on her side of the bed, worried that she'd hopped a train or hitched a ride in search of the next adventure.

9. Remember the first time you tried to buy butcher's twine in the supermarket to secure Justine in place. They didn't have it in stock. The sales associate looked at you like you were an idiot for even asking. You chose duct tape instead of your first thought: use dental floss instead. How stupid would dental floss have been? She'd either break right through it and escape, or cut her wrists and ankles to shreds trying to get free. Bloody wrists are never a good look on a girl. Cut wrists are a cliché, as sad as the runaways who burn your ears with tales of touchy stepfathers. Justine deserved better than that. The floss would have caused her pain, and that was never your intention. You wanted to keep her, not hurt her.

10. Remove the meat from the refrigerator. Allow it to sit and come to room temperature. Finish the bottle of whiskey. This should take about 30 minutes.

11. Preheat the oven to 400°F

12. Uncover and place her thigh in a large pan. Roast for 1 hour.

13. Your kitchen should be filled with a deliciously garlicky smell similar to roast pork. Reminisce about the smell of life on the road in her dirty, greasy hair as you gently kissed her head, the broken in leather from her motorcycle jacket as you kissed her neck, the combination of sweetness and alcohol on her breath from the Wild Irish Rose wine she favored as you made your way to her lips, but most importantly, focus your attention on and catch an imaginary whiff of the stale clove cigarette smoke that you'll never be able to smell again without thinking of her.

14. Improvise on the original recipe and insert 5 whole cloves into the slits in the skin. Space them apart evenly.

15. Lower the heat to 300°F and return her to the oven.

16. Allow the clove smell to bring tears to your drunken eyes. It was the right choice to deviate from the recipe and introduce the extra ingredient. The scent is beautiful. It's Justine-chain smoking Djarum and playing 25-cent video blackjack with you all night at The Peppermill when things were still good. You'd tip the worn-out cocktail waitress a $20 so she was always back as soon as you took the last sip of your bourbon and Justine polished off her vodka cran (even run down Reno grind joints, didn't serve bum wine) to hand you a fresh comp drink. When the sun came up, you'd cash out and return to your car for sloppy drunk sex and 4 hours of sleep, then wash up in the casino and start over.

17. Roast the thigh in the oven for 4 hours and get some drunk sleep.

18. Use a fork to prick the meat. Make certain to use a meat thermometer to ensure the innermost part of the thigh reaches 185°F. If a bit of the crust falls off and the meat shreds, it's finished.

19. Allow the meat to rest on the counter for 20 minutes before carving.

20. Meanwhile, go to the basement. Wake the new Justine by poking her with the fork. Use your chef's knife to cut through the duct tape. Embrace her, taking special care to hold the back of her head tight to your chest. This will make her feel safe with you. Kindly ask her to

wash up and wear that tartan mini skirt, leather jacket and denim vest you adore her in. Dinner will be ready when she is.

21. Pour a bottle of Wild Irish Rose into a 16oz glass for her. You should probably drink water after all the whiskey from earlier in the day. Compromise and pop open a can of light beer.

22. Use a carving knife to remove the outer crust. Gently slice Justine away from her bone. Plate the shredded meat with a piece of the crust on top. Punch the wall for forgetting to make a side of rice. Blame the Evan Williams.

23. Take a deep breath. Feel around for that engagement ring the first Justine was wearing when you met her at the bus terminal in New York. Make sure it's in your pocket. Check again to make double sure.

24. Run a comb through your hair. Queue the record up. Sit at your side of the table with a welcoming smile on your face as you await this Justine's arrival.

25. This one is special. This one is different. You just know it.

Contributors

Matt Andrew is a recently retired U.S. Marine officer with multiple deployments in support of combat operations in Afghanistan and the Balkans. He currently lives and works near Dallas, Texas. His fiction also appears in Pantheon Magazine, Dark Moon Digest, and Bete Noir, and is upcoming with Eldritch Press.

Angel Luis Colón's fiction has appeared in multiple online and print journals like Shotgun Honey, The Flash Fiction Offensive, Revolt Daily, Thuglit, and All Due Respect. His debut novella, 'The Fury of Blacky Jaguar' is due out this summer from One Eye Press.

Mathew Allan Garcia is the publisher of Pantheon Magazine. His fiction has been published or is forthcoming at Goldfish Grimm's Spicy Fiction Sushi, Solarcide, and NewMyths.com, among others. You can follow him on Twitter @sound879

Paul J. Garth has had fiction published in Needle, Thuglit, Blight Digest, Shotgun Honey, and Thrills, Kills, 'n Chaos, as well as a story in the anthology "Trouble in the Heartland: Crime Fiction Inspired by the Songs of Bruce Springsteen." He lives and writes in Nebraska, where he is finishing his first short story collection and beginning a novel.

Grant Jerkins is the author of A Very Simple Crime, At the End of the Road, and The Ninth Step. His newest novel, Done in One (with Jan Thomas), is available from St. Martin's Press/ Thomas Dunne Books. He lives with his wife and son in the Atlanta area.

W. P. Johnson is a writer of horror, weird fiction, and noir. He graduated from Temple University with a degree in English Literature and has been published by One Buck Horror, Kraken Press, Shroud, Dark Moon Books, Perpetual Motion Machine Publishing, Pulp Modern, Fox Spirit Books, Dark House Press, and Thunderdome Press. You can follow him on social media through the moniker americantypo. He currently lives and works in Philadelphia and is working on his first novel.

John Leahy is the author of two novels, CROGIAN and The Faith. In 2015 and 2016 Permuted Press will release his novels The Boy Who Came Back To Earth and One Step Ahead. When not writing John Leahy spends his time teaching and performing music, working out, and keeping abreast of the stock market and current affairs. He lives in Abbeyfeale in County Limerick, Ireland.

Eddie McNamara is a NYC based writer and chef. His writing has appeared in Penthouse, Thuglit, J Journal, Shotgun Honey, All Due Respect and a bunch of other grimy places. Check out his vegetarian recipes at tossyourownsalad.tumblr.com

J.M. Perkins is an action horror author, freelance game designer, and writer of other things. He is strict vegan alt health worker by day, carnivorous hard living husband/father by night. He knows... he confuses himself too. He is represented by Eliza Rothstein at Inkwell Literary Management Agency.

Joe Powers is a Canadian horror writer with a fondness for literary sleight-of-hand. He loves the idea of prompting a strong emotional reaction using no more than words and his slightly off-center imagination, and delights in taking the reader on journeys to previously unexplored regions. He is a member of ArtsLink NB, the Writers' Federation of New Brunswick, the NB Authors Portal and the Short Fiction Writers' Guild, and is active in the local arts and writing communities. His work has appeared in several anthologies and magazines. You can follow Joe at www.joepowersauthor.com

Multiple award-winning author, **Jacqueline Seewald**, has taught creative, expository and technical writing at Rutgers University as well as high school English. She also worked as both an academic librarian and an educational media specialist. Fifteen of her books of fiction have been published to critical praise including: THE INFERNO COLLECTION, THE DROWNING POOL, THE TRUTH SLEUTH, DEATH LEGACY, THE THIRD EYE and THE BAD WIFE. Her short stories, poems, essays, reviews and articles have appeared in hundreds of diverse publications and numerous anthologies such as THE WRITER, L.A. TIMES, PEDESTAL, SHERLOCK HOLMES MYSTERY MAGAZINE, OVER MY DEAD BODY!, GUMSHOE REVIEW, LIBRARY JOURNAL, and PUBLISHERS WEEKLY.

John Steele was born and bred in Belfast, Northern Ireland , and has lived anywhere they'd have him since leaving university, including the US, eastern Europe and the Far East. After fooling his wife into marriage, he moved to England where he writes and spends too much time yelling at twenty-two men kicking a leather ball around a grass field on TV. He has had several short stories published and is currently looking for a publisher for his first novel, a violent thriller set in Belfast.

Tony Wilson was born in the vast wasteland of the Midwest. He was raised on a steady diet of classic TV shows, horror comics, video games, and drive-in movies. He is a repository for useless trivia. Hobbies include writing, reading comics, roleplaying games, and weaving chainmail. He currently lives in North Carolina with his wife and two crazy dogs.

Editors

Frank Larnerd was born in Knoxville, Tennessee and spent much of his childhood engrossed in weird stories of monsters, mutants, and other worlds. He has worked as a morgue night watchman, shoe salesman, and color commentator for IWA: East Coast wrestling. Although he is best known for his unique blend of traditional Appalachian folklore and unsettling horror, Frank has also published numerous science fiction and crime stories.

Currently, Frank studies Professional Writing at West Virginia State University, where he has received multiple awards for fiction and non-fiction.

He lives in Putnam County, West Virginia.

Bracken MacLeod lives in New England and has worked as a martial arts teacher, a university philosophy instructor, for a children's non-profit, and as a criminal and civil trial attorney. While he tries to avoid using the law education, he occasionally finds uses for the martial arts and philosophy training. His stories have appeared in Sex and Murder Magazine, Every Day Fiction, Femme Fatale: Erotic Tales of Dangerous Women, Reloaded: Both Barrels Vol. 2, and Ominous Realities from Gray Matter Press. His debut novel, MOUNTAIN HOME, is available from Books of the Dead Press on Amazon and Barnes and Noble, and his novella, WHITE KNIGHT, is available from One Eye Press.

Jan Kozlowski is a freelance writer, editor and researcher. Her first novel DIE, YOU BASTARD! DIE! was published in 2012 by John Skipp's Ravenous Shadows imprint. Her short stories have appeared in HUNGRY FOR YOUR LOVE: An Anthlogy of Zombie Romance and FANGBANGERS: An Erotic Anthology of Fangs, Claws, Sex and Love, both edited by Lori Perkins, and in NECON EBOOKS FLASH FICTION ANTHOLOGY BEST OF 2011. You can visit her at JanKozlowski.com.

Ron Earl Phillips lives nestled in the foothills of West Virginia with his wife, daughter and one too many cats. He is the publisher and managing editor of One Eye Press, and is responsible for Shotgun Honey (Crime), The Big Adios (Western), and Blight Digest (Horror). He has been known to write. Find out more at RonEarlPhillips.com.

Thank you for reading

BLIGHT
Winter 2015   DIGEST

please visit us online
www.blightdigest.com